1

Laura Clark grew up in Gloucestershire and studied music at the University of Birmingham. Highlights of her musical career include singing at St Peter's Basilica and getting a fork for Gareth Malone's couscous, before he was really famous. She has written for: Musical Opinion, San Francisco Classical Voice, New Humanist, BBC Music Magazine's news feed, Jazz Journal, Warships International Fleet Review, Drama and Theatre, CBeebies magazine, The Wotton Times, Good on Paper and others. Her children's story book 'A Conker for a Pearl' was made into a stop-motion animation by Sasha Langford and screened at InMotion Festival in Aberdeen.

She is currently working on a new novel – the title is one word this time.

For the mad ones. And the dad one.

For all my friends, family, fans and everyone that knows and loves me, DJ, because farck knows if I'll finish another one.

'We are all born mad. Some remain so.'

~Samuel Beckett~

September 6th, 2019 – Dr Jonathan Nylon (Lecturer in History)

And we're off. Off our heads to be back here again.

Opening buffet ceremony was disappointing. Dr Branston and his cronies cleaned out the tower of sausage rolls and Prof Singh's homemade curry in under ten mins. So I had to settle for a meagre plate of cheese and pineapple on sticks and a few broken salt and vinegar Pringles.

I don't like to speak ill of the living, but he is the spitting image of Jeremy Bentham. I don't like to speak ill of the dead either, so a living comparison is probably not ideal – Jeremy in his pickled state maybe, pickled in urine. If only Dr Branston came with a glass case encircling his head as well, like our philosophical mate at the Royal College of Surgeons, I wouldn't have to suffer his foul breath on a regular basis. He has a very ghostly pallor these days, I don't think he's been anywhere nice on his holidays. We'll never know, I wouldn't like to ask – he has a smorgasbord of unpleasant habits, two of which are talking with his mouth full and talking at length.

There was a new female member of staff in attendance, an extremely attractive woman. dressed in a knee length black knitted dress and patent boots. Her eyes were darting about a lot (and not in the direction of the buffet table like the rest of the contingent). Every now and then she would sharply raise her head, like a startled thoroughbred. What's brought her to this knacker's yard of an institution, I don't know.

6 pm – found a fly inside the fridge this evening – affixed to a miniature pot of Domino's Garlic and Herb Dip. Dated 2001. I'll have to talk to Kyle again.

2 am – woken up in the night by a very vivid dream involving Dr Branston and the new female staff member. Dr Branston was the maître d' at a Victorian brothel. (I'm aware brothels do not have maître d's but alas – the unconscious is a curious beast!) The scene then cut to the female staff member in her patent boots, surrounded by a hazy red mist. An abundance of sausage rolls in various states of collapse and degradation lay at her feet. It was like Van Dyck meets Francis Bacon – perhaps over a game of Pictionary at a party hosted by Adriaen Brouwer.

I'm no dream analysis expert, but I suspect the red mist is not good. I'm clearly still feeling bitter about the buffet. It is the same story every year. Old wounds don't heal!

September 6th – Dr Molly Beaujolais (Lecturer in Performing Arts and Applied Theatre)

I'll give it a term. I think the worst is over. The sausage rolls are all gone. 'They are gone. They are gone to feed the roses.' A dirge without music. Some occasions are best enjoyed in non-companionable silence though. There's no way I would want Dr Branston jostling up against me during *Oops Upside Your Head*!

OH GOD!!! NO. No good-looking men. At. All!!!!!!!!!!

September 7th– Dr Jonathan Nylon

Caught up on Victoria Derbyshire show on iPlayer The producer makes some very odd musical choices. Surely a Pink Panther pastiche is not the right accompaniment for a run-down of Boris Johnson's political machinations. It did lead me to fantasize about Kato popping out and assassinating him though – perhaps that is the desired effect.

No other news of note – political or personal. The country is trapped in an irreversible hiatus and so is my social/sex life. I am in a permanent state of prorogation. My sex life has made like Kenneth Clarke and lost the whip, but not the will (not that the whip was ever in my possession, I hasten to add!). He too tried to be an upstanding member and was laughed out of office. Well, removed from office – I'm sure Chief Administrator McKinney would relish that opportunity, but I've clung on 'til now! Thank goodness, touch wood – touch the new oak floorboards, which probably cost 70 per cent of the treasurer's annual budget! Apparently, they found a "community" of brown rats below the old, gnawed ones, with a large population located under my office. Not surprising, I've had no romantic goings on in there then – the overall effect is less Playboy Mansion and more sylvan semi.

Beans on toast for tea – with a side of expired Garlic and Herb Dip. Is garlic an aphrodisiac? Think that's enough Victoria Derbyshire for one day.

September 7th – Dr Molly Beaujolais

I have just spent two hours (under Joleen's strict instruction) filling in an unnervingly detailed BDSM sexual preferences test (20 per cent 'vanilla' and 80 per cent 'exhibitionist' apparently) which has set me back in my preparations for my date tonight with François (aka a man from the internet). I predict Joleen's on the 'dominant' spectrum. If you don't want to torture and maim people, you're not going to survive dating in 2019. Well, might be some truth in that – I've had to resist the urge to use the hand-to-the-nose police defence manoeuvre on several occasions! I then spent the following two minutes talking to Mr McKinney, the admin bloke. Einstein was right when he said time is relative. Alec's cross examination was ten times as thorough as the two-hour BDSM test and he pulled it off in a fraction of the time – and himself, probably; he seemed very excited, and like multi-tasking and efficiency would rank high in his skill set.

Apparently, I'm not allowed to drink, smoke or urinate on the oak floors. So, I'm guessing I can piss freely into my desk drawer and christen my filing cabinet with Crémant any time I like.

8 pm – I have just returned from my date with François. Note the time. Disaster. I'm ashamed to say that I saw him, and he wasn't wearing a woollen hat in real life, and it wasn't a good look for him. Made me think of when my optician had hair implants, and they were so painful he could only have two strands. 'Are they darker like this or like this – which one is darker, the first or the second?' he said – moving in and out of the strip light, strands wafting gently as he went. 'They're much of a muchness,' I said. 'They've done a good job of matching up the colours.'

Going with Mum's analogy that online dating is like shopping for puppies, this one needed an urgent trip to Rolf Harris's *Animal Hospital* – or maybe not?!

He looked like he'd been through enough! A puppy with no fur and in need of a home – he kept asking me if I have a spare room. Not for him. Nan would not be happy about a Frenchman manhandling her Toby jugs.

I'd say it's more of an overpriced auction for traumatised lab rats than a puppy sale. I include myself in that analogy: 'we are all in the gutter' and 'we are all queens', to quote French Eurovision contestant Bilal Hassani, as he did, frequently throughout the evening. Some of us are more Turandot than Targaryen, although he did have Princess Beatrice's teeth to his credit, so maybe some royal blood down the line.

He fired multiple geography questions at me after I hesitated over the capital of Bulgaria – it wasn't worth a plate of patatas bravas and some cheap Rioja I tell you! Not sure how much left I've got in my arsenal for this shit. After an hour I pretended I had to pick up my children and had forgotten. He said, 'From where?' And I said, 'The pub.' It was the first thing that came into my head.

September 8th – Dr Jonathan Nylon

Spring cleaned the flat from top to bottom. I feel like Aggie and/or Kim – who have apparently been locked in a ten-year feud, would you have it! I'm sure the sight of my flat would repair the severed bonds of friendship, as they remember their shared values of cleanliness and ... gosh, not sure what else they have in common really? Hair pieces? Oh no, that's just one of them – Aggie/Kim – they're sort of interchangeable in the public eye, yet worlds apart. Not surprising they fell out really.

I have: swept the MDF floorboards (no oak for me!), applied the (faulty) hoover to them and manually extracted Kyle's hair from the carpet that the hoover rejected; rebagged and removed a decomposing sea bass carcass from the floor into the bin; 'cleaned' the bathroom (for as long as I could stomach); ditto the section of the hall outside Kyle's room; washed bed linen (is that phrase still used?); rejigged the paintings that we inherited from the landlord, not purchased by me – just for clarification (I've put the one with the solitary man in a glass-fronted bar above the sofa and the strange Picasso one with the monkey and the child I've put behind it – gives me the heebie-jeebies for some reason). Think it's down to a scene I witnessed at Bristol Zoo at a tender age involving two seemingly ill-suited prosimians and a half-eaten banana. Not the introduction to the birds and the bees I had hoped for at 13! My mother was so put out, we left post-haste, and I didn't get to see the wild fowl and mini-beast enclosure.

September 8th – Dr Molly Beaujolais

Can't write. Can't move. Can't find love.

Can't get off Instagram ... it's for research purposes, trying to connect with the students, etc, etc.

I only endure the pain of missing you

and knowing I can't hug you because

I can't eat these miles twixt you and I

neither can I drink the vast Ocean dry

@ihosiana

Unless the ocean is made of Rioja and I'm on a beach date with François, then I could knock it back. Fancy a Twix now. A boyfriend could get up and get you a Twix. Fuck's sake.

11 pm – forgot to put my washing from last night in the dryer, so I'm sleeping on a bed with no sheets – and no man between them.

September 9th – Dr Jonathan Nylon

Kyle flew into my room this morning in a blind rage saying I'd thrown away his vintage collection of fast-food condiments. Apparently, he's been collecting them for months for an art installation piece he's working on. I wondered what all those little gaffer-taped packages were – in a way I'm relieved. I had suspected he was running a mail order drug service from our humble abode! He also accused me of locking him out of the house. Not true. He claims I held the handle until he got bored and went to stay at his girlfriend's house. Again, I explained, that is an inaccuracy – I held the other end of the door handle because I just so happened to be leaving the premises at exactly the same time. In truth, I did hold on a little longer than your average exit: perhaps if you'd forgotten something and then had an existential crisis and forgotten to let go of the handle whilst lost in your thoughts – then it wouldn't be too abnormal.

I suppose an equivalent scene would be if two people/staunch enemies met in the street and had that awkward/congenial conundrum over which way to turn, but instead of it being swiftly resolved, one person decided to stay adhered to the other's footsteps and proceeded to move in a rotary motion like a fencer circling his opponent. That is of course a hyperbolic comparison, I've been reading a 'coming of age' novel by a man called Steve Barstow lately for some reason (I think that's his name, or Steve Barstool as I like to think of him) – not interesting enough to have a drink named after him. A quick Google has led me to discover that he has been supplanted in recent times by a man with the same name who travels the world looking for vegetables. Barstow the original must be disappointed. Another gift from the landlord, along with the other 1970s relics that populate our bookshelf. He's brought out an ostentatious side in me – Steve, not the landlord, who only aggravates my servile tendencies. Anyhow, I digress. The long and winding road that leads me to the door, back to the door story. And unfortunately back to Kyle. It was a rare moment for me to enjoy some power over him and I was admittedly a bit reluctant to relinquish it – he undoubtedly rules the roost in this hell house. I was Jacob wrestling with the angel, and I'm pleased to say the creature possessing the most humanity won.

Student register tomorrow. When will it end! The angels are punishing me.

September 9th – Dr Molly Beaujolais

I spoke to Nan today. She has just docked in the Caribbean. She seemed fairly oblivious to hurricane Dorian but was well aware that they would be leaving early and not getting their "money's worth". I could hardly hear a word she was saying, she had a mouth full of Rum Baba. She has met a new man by the sound of it. That and it's "fucking hot". She said she's had nothing but goat curry, and her arse is like a hot coin. She has a mouth like a sewer, I don't know how a clean-living American like Tab Hunter put up with it! I think their brief 'love affair' in the summer of 1966 was purely a personal PR stunt, one that never made the papers thankfully – I wouldn't trust Nan at an awards ceremony, 'Cat Ballou' – Grizabella Bellowing more like! Thank the Lord he was invested enough in the charade to invest in a two-bed apartment in Maida Vale. I would have to sell a kidney and a lung and take up a career as an internationally acclaimed heart surgeon to pay for this gaff now.

Looking forward to the students registering next week at the moment – it will be nice to speak to some young people/some people. I haven't spoken to anyone besides Nan all day. I feel like a geriatric who ought to be enrolled in Age UK's 'combatting loneliness' scheme.

September 10th – Dr Jonathan Nylon

Students are enrolling on the 16th!! I got the dates wrong. Turned up to an empty campus! Actually, that's not strictly true, I think I saw Mr McKinney skulking about in the Tudor Maze; I made it into the safe haven of Queen's courtyard just in time. There was an awkward moment when we both had to watch the electric gate closing between us, but thankfully we were just far away enough that embarking on a conversation would've been a strain for a man with limited hearing such as himself. I hope he understands. And that he knows how to operate the electric gate! He was still standing there in that same position for a good 15 seconds after the gate had closed.

Seeing as I was out and about and possibly to accrue some karmic points after abandoning Mr

McKinney at the school gates, I dipped into McDonald's on the way home, to harvest some dips from their ample stocks for Kyle. I guessed correctly that they would have a variety of vintages available! It was a very awkward scene, families eyeing me as if I was some kind of sauce fetishist – perhaps I should have bought something. I hope he will express his gratitude by cleaning the ketchup stains from the ceiling that have been there for several weeks now.

September 10th – Dr Molly Beaujolais

Joleen has decided we're going away to Barcelona for three nights – I said I've got lecture plans to write, but she said, in her broad Lancashire drawl, 'You can do that with a Sangria in hand and a man between your thighs.' So, it's booked and we're setting off tomorrow at three am! EasyJet.

September 11th – Dr Jonathan Nylon

Parliament has been prorogued – the lights have gone down in the halls of Westminster. I went to Westminster library to get my affairs in order for Monday. It took me all afternoon and a fair portion of the evening to rifle through the student mug shots and draft out a few lecture plans. Key themes are sex and death. I always come back to these, like a homing pigeon. I should have been a journalist. Libraries are odd places, aren't they? I saw a woman of indeterminable age and wearing one of those wolf jumpers you have no idea where people buy, longitudinally lounging in the Geography section. I had to almost step over her to get to the Medieval History section, where I encountered a gentleman (old enough to know better!) filing his nails over a copy of *Medicine in the Middle Ages* – it was enough to give you a hot stomach!

I made a detour via the park on the way home, they've set up an allotment there. Tesco Express has competition, and they go by the name of The Forest Hill Foragers and Growers Society. I peered over the fence and there was a jovial crowd of badly aged characters, sharing hearty jokes, sloshing down hot drinks from flasks in between ploughing the land. It truly was a bucolic scene, worthy of one of Brouwer's more light-hearted works.

I was greeted by the stale whiff of 'medieval' fried chicken as I walked through the door (as opposed to the homely aroma of turnip stew the allotment revellers will no doubt be enjoying). Kyle is working nights at 'The Medieval Banquet' at the moment. You'd have thought he would have had enough of the stuff! It took me an hour to extract a poultry bone from the washing machine the other day. I wish he wouldn't bring his work home with him.

He was in one of his rare convivial moods this evening, telling me about how the town crier character from the Banquet has found a full-time job in finance, so they all had to take it in turns in their 30-minute breaks to ring the bell. I said they could ask that bloke at Westminster shouting at all hours of the day to audition – he'd have to adapt his chant of 'stop Brexit' to chime with the rhythm of 'bring out your dead' though. I took the opportunity to present him with the sauce pots I'd foraged. His reaction was less than enthusiastic. He turned over one of the pots, looked at the sell by date and said, 'Rupi Kaur didn't use the word 'wept' in 2015.' I don't know who that is, Diary – maybe she had a happy year. But the tension was already too high to ask. And then to rub salt into the wound, monosodium glutamate into a ketchup marinade, he gestured to a Wilko's carrier bag and said, 'I've just bought a coffee machine, it was really expensive, I don't really want other people using it.' By other people I'm guessing he means me as I'm the only other person who lives here. 'Ah right,' I said. I took my cold tea and went off to hide in my room for 12 hours.

9 pm – checked the news – Parliament has been de-prorogued. A silver lining on this grey day!

September 12th – Dr Jonathan Nylon

7 am – it's time to wake up and smell the fresh coffee. A sniff is all I'll ever get.

September 13th – Dr Jonathan Nylon

Very refreshing drink at the Sylvan Post with George this evening. Spent the morning gazing agonisingly at the coffee machine. That 9th century Ethiopian goatherd has brought more harm than good into the world by inventing it (coffee that is, not the machine – although the Abyssinian Empire was very industrious, I wouldn't put it past them). George was telling me all about his recent adventures as a tabloid junior journalist. He's been partnered with an abrasive sounding senior journalist called Demelza, who has a different coloured Topshop trouser suit for each day of the week. Yesterday it was pink with yellow polka dots – they had to 'do a death knock' in Hither Green, about a 17-year-old Taiwanese boy who has gone missing in Kuwait. 'I had to hang back for my own safety Johnny, it was like watching Mr Blobby on one of his tirades, press-ganging the public into revealing information that they don't have about Noel Edmunds! She forced me to approach this poor old man in his garden. I pretended he was deaf, and she said to me,

'What? You haven't even spoken to him.' I said, 'He looks the type,' and she seemed satisfied with that, saying she'll "come for him later", and then we went to get a latte in Starbucks.'

He looked into his martini and bitter lemon a bit forlornly, so I tried to chivvy him up by saying it's a great achievement to have a full-time job at a national newspaper (I left out 'tabloid'). It's a bit like when your friend starts going out with an absolute knobhead, but you can't say anything until they break up. 'We've come a long way from French boys firing cap guns into our ears at Camp Soleil,' I said.

'Well, you have.'

September 14th – Dr Molly Beaujolais

I am now sober enough to hold a pen. We're on the plane home and not speaking. I think more from exhaustion than hostility, but I don't know if I'll ever be able to say for sure. We've lived through a lot together.

I think it would be best if we spent our days from now on in companionable/non-companionable silence.

There are four characters in this commedia dell'arte: me, Joleen, Pablo and Goar. Joleen and I were omnipresent on stage, and I think this may have been the driving force for the dramatic tension.

We met Pablo and Goar at the Irish bar on the first night and that was the beginning of the end for our cultural excursion. Goar wrote his name on Joleen's arm in Max Factor scarlet lip gloss and our fates were sealed (you need a very astringent make-up remover to get that stuff off, hours of scrubbing with a cotton pad – you're better off going for a quick slick of turps). Goar is pronounced gŏa like a Cockney saying 'phwoar'. Joleen's swarthy señor was always plying her with honeyed sweet Spanish nothings; they texted continually. Pablo didn't text, but he knew where to find me – in the Irish bar after dark. Theirs was a meeting of minds, our relationship was more physical and could only be conducted under the influence of alcohol.

Goar had a low-slung forehead perched on top of kindly eyes. Pablo had more going for him in the forehead department, but a mealy mouth you could imagine turning into a snarl if his tapas came out cold. But their hearts were in the right place, even if their facial features were not. Goar usually had a carafe of sangria and two espressos waiting for me and Joleen (I think we might have banged on a bit too much about how tired we were from all the walking/sightseeing). It was quite a cosy and domesticated set up by day two – #hygge

I mentioned Pablo to Mum, and she said we should go to a museum together. So, at 11 pm, at the bar I tried out some of my Spanish GCSE lingo on Pablo: 'Vamos al museo?' He looked at his watch and said, 'No we go to your house?' with a quizzical eyebrow raise.

As may potentially be the case in death, we made it to the Gaudi gates of many a cathedral and garden of Paradise but couldn't get in: €17 is a bit steep for glimpsing heaven. And all our resources needed to be reserved for replenishing cortados and evening escapades with Bunce and Bean. It was grating on me a bit that Joleen wanted to spend every waking moment lazing on the shores of La Barceloneta and crawling the beach bars. We already had Pablo and Goar! What we didn't have was an instagrammable photo of the interior of the Sagrada Familia.

I managed to prize her fingers away from a 'Long Sloe Uncomfortable Screw' for long enough for us to reach the summit of the Joan Miró Museum. We didn't make it inside. 'I can't believe we've walked all the way up this bloody hill to see ET with his kecks down, he's not going home in that right state!' she said. 'Joan Miró? If I wanted to see some old English lady's perverted art, I could've gone to see my aunt Sarah in Abbey Village, she's always making minging sculptures in her glass blowing class.'

We had a good laugh about the phallus-like structures and the one that looked like one of the mangled toys from *Toy Story*, but it was a relief to get out into open uncultured space where we could be our wicked selves again.

The drama reached its apex on the final night. A heated Brexit debate, which culminated in a *Thelma and Louise* style journey along the harbour pier, a pied (stilettoed pied). When we reached the edge, the debate raged on:

'People are sick of EU bureaucrats and chlorinated chickens ruling the roost,' she said.

'It's the people and the poorest people who will be hit the hardest,' I said.

'You don't know that!'

'Look, I think it would be best for both of us if we just put the conversation on hold for a bit, get a drink and consult BBC News.'

'It's been going on for three years, we need it to be done away with now!'

'You can't do away with Europe! Whatever happened to love your neighbour – we've been in peacetime for forty years, people take that for granted.'

'Ay? More like sixty?!'

'I always round down to the millennium.'

Then I said, 'What about the NHS and the farming communities?'

And that, darling diary, is the last thing I remember saying before she grabbed me and thrust me into the icy waters of the Mediterranean Sea! Apparently, she was trying to bring an end to the debate with a dramatic embrace, but we'll never really know. I knew I was going to regret venturing out in those five-inch heels, but I'd brought them, so I was going to wear them at least once. But it's not fair to blame the Topshop Saskia Snake Skinny 2 Parts when really Brexit is the root cause. All this civil unrest – sister turning against sister. Wrapped in a silver thermal blanket on the beach, my teeth were chattering so much I could hardly talk but we both managed to apologise for the hurtful things we'd said about each other's Latin lovers: that Goar has a spherical head like Phil Mitchell and Pablo looks like a Spanish Jacob Rees-Mogg. Goar was present and in ear shot, but his English is quite limited, so I think it was fine. It certainly hasn't dampened his affections for Joleen, he's texting her as I write this (we have just landed in Gatwick). I confessed to Joleen that Pablo and I might have a future after Barcelona, we have some things in common, theatre for example – he works as a technician at the Flamenco City Hall. 'No babe,' she said, 'he works at the construction site with Goar.'

On the beach, Goar loomed his Gaudi head in between us and said, 'Pablo is sorry, he's not here. He had to work late.' He couldn't pull the wool over my eyes anymore! I knew where he'd be, where he always was – at the Irish bar. The scales, the crane, had been lifted! I hoped not though – it was very poorly lit in that area by the construction site. I was angry, but I didn't wish him a sticky end (of any description! Not anymore!)

Buena suerte to them both and good luck to me and Joleen in salvaging our friendship.

September 15th – Dr Jonathan Nylon

Saw that female staff member in Regent's Park today, she was with a woman with half a shaved head, a black pug and a silvery grey Great Dane. Her natural red hair was being blown about madly by the wind, which gave her the look of one of Brouwer's fairer maidens. I gave a little head nod and small wave, and she bowed her head gracefully and smiled.

Discovered a new coffee shop by campus. They exclusively sell bagels and records – and coffee! There are empty jars of used marmite on the windowsills and arty magazines you've never heard of. They play a game of trying to guess the musical references in the songs playing. It's very cool. I think I'm going to request a gramophone for the office.

Snippets from David Cameron's biography were all over the news yesterday. No doubt a great deal of agonising went on in Waterstones across the country over whether to stock the hard-boiled hardbacks in fiction or non-fiction. He's come out saying 'some leavers had left the truth at home on the campaign trail' (like a forgotten flask) and that he thinks about the referendum "every day". I think this is called projection. Tomorrow I will be trying to project that I'm thinking about my students during the personal tutor sessions, but I will really be thinking about acquiring a gramophone and coffee machine for my office. What a web of lies we all weave!

2 am – dreamt about the new female staff member again. She was riding a Great Dane and wearing a crown reminiscent of Queen Matilda's. I was riding the pug and trying to keep up with her as she crossed a drawbridge into her high security castle. Another vision of foreboding!

September 16th – Dr Jonathan Nylon

Tuesday I got the wrong date. Today I got the wrong institution, because I turned up and there were a load of 12 year-olds waiting to register. Am I ancient now? I found a single white hair growing out of my back this morning! Shooting out of a mole like the gleaming sword of Excalibur – undiscovered and untouched for 883 years.

I managed to grab a bourbon and a pink wafer before rushing to my office for the 'personal tutor' 1:1 meetings, 1 and 1 indeed! One (coffee machine coffee deprived being) and a host of absent beings. They all look in urgent need of a blood transfusion and/or a pint! Was I this wan and unenthused as a young undergraduate?!

It wasn't easy getting through them with the racket going on next door! I'm sure I heard a cat's meow at one point and scratching on the wall – he'll have McKinney after him if he vandalises university property. What sort of personal counsel is Dr M Beaujolais offering his students – primal scream sessions by the sounds of it, in the manner of Rafiki (if he had decided to abandon the ways of the old religion in favour of modern psychology). The student made a convincing cat in his defence, but the illusion was shattered when he started going on about how many men he'd slept with. I don't remember that happening in Andrew Lloyd Webber's masterpiece.

I have a student who wants to base her thesis on her own family history. She felt inspired by Danny Dyer's story on *Who Do You Think You Are?* and his follow up series, *Right Royal Family.* I said, 'What is your family's history?' She said they were dockers in the East End.

'And before that?'

'They were Irish farmers.'

I didn't have the heart to tell her, but that is usually the part in the show where viewers tune out. We discussed the merits of Daniel Radcliffe's story versus Sharon Osbourne's, then I gave her a weak smile and wordlessly handed her a timetable.

I am hanging by a finger from a branch of the philosophical tree to reference Martin Heidegger quoting Descartes, writing to Picot, and I am ready for the metaphysical roots to take me down into the earth.

September 16th – Dr Molly Beaujolais

Oh dear, I don't know what the fuck I'm going to do with these students – they're running for the hills already, but not Julie Andrew's hills – alive with musical and theatrical opportunity. More like a modest country hillock, followed by a very steep ravine.

My first personal tutor session overran by half an hour. I had a student who wants to transfer to a Music Theatre course at the Royal Academy of Music. Most of the session was taken up with him mewling like a cat (he is planning on auditioning for Deuteronomy). I won't tell him that during the last performance I saw of *Cats* in that venue, a man called out 'biscuits' at frequent intervals and did a warbling impersonation of his chosen role several decibels louder than the orchestra and cast put together.

I made him a cup of tea and gave him the handful of biscuits I'd scavenged from the foyer. He is worried about his love life and making it in the bizz – my heart breaks for these desperate souls. He dreams of being admired like a sphinx, but he'll probably end up an old street cat like the rest of us. I told him there is a place for everyone on this path unwinding, to which he snapped, 'I don't want to play Mufasa!' I wish I'd kept back some of the pink wafers now.

I'm going to have to get these walls insulated. Don't want Dr Jonathan Nylon getting his suspenders in a twist, he sounds the type!

September 17th – Dr Jonathan Nylon

Popped into Tesco to purchase some Blu Tack – the recycling instructions need reaffixing onto the fridge. Kyle keeps dislodging them with his greasy, medieval banquet covered fingers. I needed the help of three different shop assistants to pass the purchase through the self-checkout. I dread to think how I will fare as an elderly person in this machine-driven age. In my defence, the problem was down to an abandoned basket of cigarettes and alcohol and not my tech skills – Noel Gallagher's perhaps, deciding all he needed was actually to vacate the shop immediately and escape the self-checkout induced saga. When I returned home, I saw the dozens of sauce pots I had collected for Kyle haplessly strewn about the floor by the bins. The foxes must have got at them and had a saucy feast, because there is no way Kyle would have washed them out. He has won the battle, but he will not win the war!

2 am – I have done a mad thing. I have gone out into the night, with the sound of mating foxes resounding in my ear like sirens calling me to the rocks – the rocks of insanity! Kyle's spirit animal coaxing me to dash my weary head no doubt. I collected the pots and I've displayed them in the kitchen in a formation resembling the initial phase of the first Battle of Narvik. I think it's pre-term nerves.

September 18th – Dr Molly Beaujolais

A student invited me to a foam party this afternoon – I said, 'I shall be having a foam party of my own tonight, alone in the bath with a glass of red wine.' I hoped it would indicate I lead a very boring and lonesome life, but it had the opposite effect I fear, as he then asked if he could join me.

I'm still yet to meet my neighbour, Dr Jonathan Nylon – sounds a bit like a 1970s serial killer, perhaps one that works part time at a knicker factory. You would never hear him coming if he is! He's as silent as the grave. I did overhear his name in the canteen yesterday though, whilst I was waiting for my shrivelled chicken escalope and chips (I think I'm going to go vegan). A girl at the salad bar, who has a Norwegian mother and German father from what I can gather, was lamenting how he had "banged on for bloody ages" about the "geopolitical and economic benefits of warm-water ports, such as the one at the Ofotfjord, Norway's twelfth-longest fjord". 'Maybe he fancies you,' said the friend. A murderer and a pervert then!

September 19th – Dr Jonathan Nylon

When I went to make myself a cup of Yorkshire's finest this morning, I saw that Kyle had left a selection of mould-filled milk cartons displayed along the windowsill by the sink. A normal person would have emptied them into the sink and got on with their life or confronted him. However, all I could see in the marbling threads of green, white and yellow was the mottled effect of the Northern Lights dancing on the frosty glaciers of the Narvik mountains. Perhaps some of the furrier mounds pertained to the birch, pine and aspen that can be found there. Some of the contents had also found their way into the sink (representing the rich variety of marine life that inhabit one of Norway's finest fjords?) and a large clump clung to the tap like a beached orca.

Before I could stop myself, I had dashed to the recycling box and scooped up the empty sauce pots. I've moved into phase two of this manic cycle, and it is manifesting itself as the second Battle of Narvik: a necessary morale-boosting manoeuvre for the Royal Navy and a crucial strategic move for securing a

German defeat. I filled the sink and positioned Battleship HMS Warspite (Tangy BBQ) and the nine destroyers: HMS Bedouin; Cossack; Punjabi (Habanero Ranch for these classy Tribal-class vessels) and Eskimo. I was torn between using Spicy Buffalo for Eskimo (for setting Hermann Künne ablaze) or Sweet 'n' Sour for her chequered military history. HMS Kimberley, Hero, Icarus, Forester and Foxhound had to be ordinary ketchup ('signature sauce') because that's all that was left. Icarus kept getting lodged against the orca, but I don't think this mattered too much in the grand military scheme of things. To give the full effect, I balanced a couple of mayonnaise sachets on top of the door frame from our own stocks, to represent aircraft carrier HMS Furious and the biplane torpedo bomber the Fairey Swordfish. I wanted to put Swordfish (aka 'Stringbag') in a mesh laundry bag, but we didn't have any left.

Then I went to have a lie down. I hope he'll see the funny side.

September 20th – Dr Jonathan Nylon

If the funny side was an angle perceptible in a hall of mirrors at a carnival in John o' Groats, Kyle saw it about as much as a man stationed in a lighthouse in the Outer Hebrides – i.e., not at all.

Kyle saw the funny side as much as I saw the full horse during *War Horse* in a far-right hand restricted view balcony seat. If the funny side was the puppeteer's arse, which is what I saw most of, Kyle would've been sat in a front-facing, top-price-bracket stalls seat.

I felt his presence before he made it known. Even though I had my back turned, his exaggeratedly elongated torso casts a long shadow. I was in the kitchen with the lights on, but even so, it was a dark day in Narvik.

'Why is the coffee machine facing the wrong way?' he said (I had to turn it away to stop me hankering after it). He'd caught me desperately trying to swivel it to its correct position, but the rubber stoppers were not budging. The bare kitchen light bulb flickered and buzzed momentarily, like the Aldis lamp of Eidsvold signalling the German approach.

'What is all this stuff doing here?' he said, and he swept the Tribal-class flotilla aside like a petulant child defeated at chess – or Adolf mapping out Operation Weserübung on the chessboard of global warfare. More like a child though, he's very frail – he has the physique of a teenage boy, but the temperament of a fully grown Hitler.

'It needs to be recycled.'

'What the fuck is wrong with you?'

'What the fuck is right with you?!'

Then he turned to leave, but it was not meant to be. He swung open the door and the inevitable happened – 'Stringbag' crash landed. The corner of the mayonnaise sachet only lightly grazed his face, but there was a lot of blood surprisingly (he would not be a strong contender for survival at the First or Second Battle of Narvik!). Needless to say, he was **HMS** bloody furious!

Then a strange sequence of events unfolded. He grabbed Eskimo and wielded him above his head like Abraham preparing to murder his only son. I bolstered myself for a battle, but instead of striking, he opened his hand and let it fall like Ophelia relinquishing petals from her faltering fingertips. He then awkwardly curled his rigid fingers into a fist, I ducked – but he just pulled his arm down to a resting position in a manner typical of a 90s boy band. There had been no uplifting key change, however – the air was stale with angst and sour milk.

He walked away from the scene, the enemy had retreated – but for some reason, in my mind, the battle wasn't over. In another of the countless moments of madness, I grabbed Foxhound and hurled it square at the back of his head. He rounded on me and said, 'You'll regret that!' To which I replied, 'that's what Fregattenkapitän Erich Bey said.' It might be the wittiest and most enjoyable thing I have ever said, under pressure.

I wrote a whole chapter of my book afterwards. The fjord floodgates have been opened!

September 20th – Dr Molly Beaujolais

Spoke to Nan today – she was on Sanur Beach in Bali. Again, I could hardly hear her, she needs to get her phone sorted! I think the problem was partly down to the rowdy rabble of protesters in the background. She has joined the Balinese people in a peaceful protest against climate change. Her afternoon was spent making a banner out of palm branches because she didn't have the necessary materials to make a placard. She did however manage to scrawl: 'Fuck the fascists' in the corner of a man called Ketut's placard, some poor father of two. I hope her right (writing) hand was occupied with a palm leaf at the time, and the text suitably obscured – not the kind of language I'm sure Ketut would like his children to be exposed to.

September 21st – Dr Jonathan Nylon

Writing.

September 21st – Dr Molly Beaujolais

Bobby, Luce and I have decided to spend a wild weekend in the country – county Gloucestershire. A rowdy touring circus had come to town. There was a man on stilts hurling fire a few inches from children's faces and a hoard of vultures on display. An elderly Morris dancer with a haphazardly painted face approached me and asked if I could take him to the toilet. I pointed him in the direction of a 200 ft Portaloo queue. *Locomotion* had just started playing.

I met a fellow East Ender who had a Peaky Blinders haircut and danced like no one was watching – even though security didn't take their eyes off him for the whole night. They call him Beacon, as he is 'the poetic star of the East' – although it turns out he hails from Eccles in Kent, so he's taken that a bit far, I think. If the wise men followed him, they'd wind up having cake and tea with a side of cucumber sandwiches at a luxury B&B, not a night in a draughty stable with the baby Jesus. We ambled along the canal, with Beacon pointing out the wildflowers, when a gang from Birdlip threw a pint over us from the vantage point of the bridge. Beacon threw the remnants of his Amstel back at them – like a gallant troll. We kissed in the alleyway on the way to Merrywalks, before the security guard caught up with us and revealed that said remnants had whetted the head of a newborn baby reclining peacefully in a carriage. He didn't use quite such a verbose description, but it doesn't feel right writing so many expletives in a row with a Parker fountain pen.

We thought the whole thing was done and dusted, but they were waiting for us at 'Devil's Elbow' on the way back to the cottage. A portly member of the mummers' cast swung for Beacon but was no match for his 22 years of boxing training (built like a whippet he is). He ducked and sent the colourfully chequered character careering into a dry-stone wall, which then crumbled beneath his colossal gait, like powdered milk (which is probably what that baby's being fed on, he was pasty as an undercooked steak bake from Greggs). I ran from the scene with chants of 'control your boyfriend' echoing in my ear. I'd only just met the fella! Once Beacon had caught up, he showed me the stiletto-shaped wound, it was very romantic.

I think this could be the beginning of a long and passionate affair.

September 22nd – Dr Jonathan Nylon

I've made it out of the barracks (the house) to stock up on food supplies. Nipped into the library, saw Danny Dyer's book (*The World According to* ...) sitting on the shelf so I absentmindedly popped it into my bag for my student. The librarian was a bit over the top about it all, when the alarms went off – it was embarrassing enough being caught red handed with an

EastEnders' character's life story. Apparently, they've had a succession of thefts lately. I tried to explain I've been in a fragile state of mind, what with the Battle of Narvik going on, but it didn't seem to help my case.

I ducked into Bloomsbury Square Gardens for a bit, to recover from the whole ordeal. The land was arid! And strewn with cigarette butts. I need this dry spell to pass now, I don't look good in summer attire – like an overgrown Boy Scout. There was a child in the park shouting *pigeon* at the top of their lungs the whole time I was there. It felt like a personal attack. I don't think I've ever shouted like that in my life, let alone on a continuous loop for 20 minutes!

Unwound with *Antiques Roadshow*. It is a well-researched programme, historically accurate most of the time. I think I prefer *Flog It!* though. I like the live auction element.

September 22nd – Dr Molly Beaujolais

If I meet one more bloke who is either scared of me or boring in future, I'm going to give them something to be scared and bored about: force them to watch eight hours back-to-back of *Antiques Roadshow*, with the prospect of being auctioned off to one of the audience members at the end. Just watching an episode now, Anne from St Agnes's solid silver flying pig nutmeg grinder might be made by John Williams or whoever it is, but it's making me want to kill myself. Oh God, just received a dagger emoji from a gentleman called Tybalt on Tinder. Call me Romeo! Don't worry Tybalt, we'd never had made it to the third act. No word from my knight in shining Adidas trainers, Beacon. I'm giving up on all this, I can't play their game – there are too many impossible rules and regulations and it's boring as arse! Why walk into a shop, touch everything in sight, ask for every minute detail about the merchandise and when the shop assistant tries to get involved, you are completely mute, or you run for the hills, and she is left shouting 'everything is returnable' to the back of your head. None of them can be trusted not to damage the stock. They usually end up going for a similar thing from

Primark, in a less 'crazy' design, available at a more accessible price that they can wear anywhere, without fear of it 'wearing them' or someone nicking it.

8.25 pm – Oh God, I just drifted off to sleep – *Antiques Roadshow* is still on! It really is the never-ending road(show)! Had a dream that I went on a Tinder date with a man (with a smattering of hair and crooked teeth) who had prepared a collage of his sexual kinks to show me, which included farmyard animal noises, represented by a cartoon sketch of what looked like Old Major from *Animal Farm* (I think that is Anne's influence and her porcine grinder) and half of Leeds football team. We walked along Barcelona pier for a little bit, having a nice heart-to-heart. Then he suddenly said, 'I can't keep up with you' (even though we were walking at a very leisurely pace) and started running in the opposite direction! I then called after him, 'You better run' – he kept going until I woke up.

Anyway, where was I? Shopping is like dating men. Don't they know that I only work there for the staff discount, I'm not an investor for Christ's sake!

More often than not, I'm only after the cheap, heady thrill of a quick sale before closing time. If it's love at first Louboutin – that is wonderful, but rare – but you have to at least take them home and live with them a bit to find out! Anyway, what's rare is getting me over the threshold, I hate shopping. I can stand in the doorway and do a quick 180 degree scan and that's the end of it. I know what I want. Otherwise, I don't go in. That is why I've had my heart broken by so many fake Louboutins, they're hard to spot from a distance. Especially when they are running far into it.

11 pm – call from Beacon. He's coming to London tomorrow to spend the week with me. I take it all back. For now.

September 23rd – Dr Molly Beaujolais

Meeting with Head of Department Professor Veal this afternoon (he looks like Brian Blessed). There is no book to discuss. I think I managed to fob him off with the title: *Misremembered Dramatists of the Parisian Fin-de-Siècle Set* (technically not a lie) – he seems happy with that. He kept looking at his cup of tea on the desk and back to me in a desperate way, like a hostage trying to communicate with the police. I think he wanted to get on and eat his Mars bar. We both knew he'd left it too close to the mug and it would be melted in moments.

Beacon surfaced from my room and made it out to campus in the afternoon – we went to this little bagel/record shop place nearby. I can't believe he's never heard of The Beatles?! We all have our blind spots I suppose. He redeemed himself by making up a limerick for me on the spot:

There was once a girl called Molly

Who never made any man sorry

She was great bants in bed

Even though she called me Fred

I would never put her in the boot of a lorry (unless we were running from the police, it was a joke, or I needed a lift – he explained afterwards).

I think it's supposed to be a bit tongue in cheek.

10.30 pm – Email from McKinney all in capital letters, asking me to put together a humanities pub quiz with Dr Jonathan Nylon – good grief! Perhaps we can devise it by tapping out Morse code on the wall – I never see the man!

September 23rd – Dr Jonathan Nylon

I've been trying to fathom where this mania has sprung from – I think a combination of having no creative outlet as a child and no sex as an adult. No sex in my current adult state anyhow.

I saw the female staff member in the canteen today, voraciously loading a plastic pot with pasta salad – there is nothing starchy about her appearance. She was wearing a very short 1960s style pinafore type dress and looked very alluring and fresh-faced. She had her hair in a ponytail, which showed off her beautiful neck and hair.

I think she might be a Doctor of Science; she spends a lot of time with Professor Sandra Peacock, the chemistry lecturer, and has an air of intelligence about her. Perhaps I'm being misled by the white mac and wire-rimmed glasses she was wearing at the time. I'm a simple man at heart, with simple desires.

In other news, I've been asked to stage a pub quiz with Dr M Beaujolais. An odd pairing we shall make! Unlikely bedfellows – I hope people don't start to associate us with each other. Morecambe and Wise, Pavlov and his dog, Sooty and his puppeteer (maybe his producer, bit less hands-on). I can't imagine he's going to pull his weight. I'm envisaging a scene at the pub like the one in that film where the man goes mad and starts beating his chest like a gorilla and harassing the dinner guests.

He seems to be enjoying some kind of lurid affair with a Northern woman. I can hear her raucous laugh reverberating through the walls on speaker phone at all hours of the day. He can't get a word in edgeways. I can't get a word written on the page from the distraction. I have never met the man, but already I can't stand him! He clearly has no respect for the privacy of others, for mine or for this poor Lancashire lass – I know every detail of her sexual history – past, present and future imperative!

September 24th – Dr Molly Beaujolais

Met Dr Jonathan Nylon today, he came and knocked on my door. I thought he was a postgraduate! He has a very immature gait. His teeth are like individual tombstones – hopefully not a harbinger of death! He invited me to the bagel/record shop down the road for lunch tomorrow, we're going to plan our quiz.

I still don't have a topic for my book – what the heck am I going to write about?! Maybe a discursive piece about the inclusion of non-historically accurate characters in contemporary children's nativity plays, such as lobsters and 1950s rock 'n' roll stars – that's a subject that's always fascinated me.

Another revelation from Beacon, he has never heard of Dickens!! We nipped into an antiquarian bookshop near Fitzrovia on the way to Wagamama's. He pulled out a copy of *David Copperfield* off the shelf and I asked him if he was a fan. He said he used to do a few magic tricks as a child but hasn't read his biography. In fairness his Vegas show has done well, Charles' quaint Suffolk sojourner can't compete.

September 24th – Dr Jonathan Nylon

It's her!!!! Are all my dreams over? I couldn't share her with the Northern woman, I would never keep up! God, she is even more beautiful close up. Like a Monet! Oh no, that's the other way round. Like a child's sketch, my niece's mermaid depictions are largely indiscernible from every angle, but if you study them very closely you can make out some shapes pertaining to real life.

Molly. My thoughts are indiscernible when I am close to her. She told me a touching story about an East End father and grown-up son she saw on the DLR at Shadwell that morning; they hardly spoke but when they passed the old Tobacco Dock he leaned over and took hold of a bit of his son's shirt and pointed – "like he was a little boy". Apparently, it was a very tender gesture, I think if one of the Mitchel brothers took hold of my shirt (whether we were related or not) I would be alarmed. I saw a flag of St George in a window the other day and thought it had been crafted into a swastika, but it turned out to just be the window frame in the end. She sees the beauty in London's underbelly, where I can only see baseness.

She is all beauty.

September 25th – Dr Jonathan Nylon

Exchanged numbers with Molly today. I noticed that she has quite an unusual mode of communicating, she sort of starts a sentence and invites you to finish it with a pause or an ambiguous 'huh' noise, which could indicate she hasn't heard you – but it sometimes comes at the end of something she's said. I'm not sure if these are exclamations of joy, boredom or confusion from something I've said or she's said – either way I like it, I enjoy the chaos of it all (strangely, for me!), and it makes me want to keep talking to her. Once you get used to it, it's quite conspiratorial and fun, like an odd Christmas parlour game.

Dr Molly Beaujolais.

She is complete – born complete, like an Italian, as Hemingway said. She doesn't sound Italian though. She sounds like a softly spoken Artful Dodger – the Artful Dodger if he smoked 40 Silk Cut a day, which he probably did. These child stars all have troubled lives.

We are going for lunch at the bagel place later, I hope she'll be impressed.

10 pm – Dr Molly Beaujolais is the most scintillating and sexually alluring person I have ever met. And I think she may have been flirting with me. We discussed possible play options for her students at

lunch. I hope that perhaps she was casting me, in her mind, as the romantic lead. There were certainly moments when she seemed to be assessing my dramatic potential, her eyes took on the misty look of Simon Cowell when he's just about to annihilate some small child's dreams of stardom.

The favourite seems to be *Antony and Cleopatra* at the moment. She had a particularly grand staging idea for the scene with the boys fanning Cleopatra. She said she would like to be fanned by a throng of boys. I said, what about one boy instead. She said 'fine' and rolled her eyes seductively, 'I'll throw them out, into the Nile.'

'Perhaps roll out your carpet for them first, cushion the fall – like an aeroplane slide.' I don't want anyone dying for their art, even if it does mean securing Molly's unrivalled attentions. Perhaps if we could find some cupid wings large enough to fit Dr Branston, I could be persuaded.

September 25th – Dr Molly Beaujolais

Sacked off Beacon for the day. He's gone go-karting in Barking.

Had lunch with Dr N. yesterday. He is a breath of fresh air after the Pablos of this planet. If he turns out to be a serial killer, then I'm with Cleopatra: 'The stroke of death is as a lover's pinch, which hurts and is desired.'

I find his uneven teeth strangely attractive.

3 am – had a naughty dream about Dr Nylon and his teeth. Dr Nylon and his teeth combined, not him and his teeth sitting in a glass on the bedside table! We were walking in the park and then we nipped behind a Buddleia bush, and he undid the buttons on my blouse with his . . . and then I woke up and spilt my water all over the floor. Oh dear. Oh doctor. Oh Johnny.

September 26th – Dr Jonathan Nylon

Molly was off sick today, her friend Sandra told me – so I went home as well as a sort of walkout protest against disease and biology. I felt surprisingly enraged at Mother Nature. A common cold inflicted on Molly seems like a grave injustice.

I was soon called back in by McKinney for a meeting I'd forgotten about and could've done without. I've got so much to do! He was telling me how he'd booked a holiday to the Bahamas, but he wasn't able to go because of the British Airways' cancellations. He said he hasn't been on holiday in 12 years. I said I sympathised, but perhaps there is a silver lining because of Hurricane Dorian – the holiday might not have lived up to his expectations. He said there is no consolation to be had at all – he had meant to book a bus to Braemar to see his family and ended up having to spend £1200 for the Bahamas flight, £450 for five nights in an Airbnb with close proximity to the beach and on top of that he had begun to form a burgeoning friendship with the lady owner, which will now inevitably never amount to anything.

Gosh, that must have been a hard blow. He is as tight as a duck's arse. I thought it was probably a bad time to bring up the coffee machine. I will try again when he is in a more robust mood.

9 pm – sent Molly a text enquiring about her general welfare and how the play research is coming along. She is favouring a stage adaption of *Lady Chatterley's Lover* now, and I seemed to have taken on the role of cuckolded husband. Some third wheel gamekeeper type character kept cropping up every two minutes, with "a body like David Gandy". I think she has deviated too much from the original text, they didn't have protein shakes in D. H Lawrence's time.

'When the husband is away – the gamekeeper enters,' she said.

'Well, he won't be away, he'll be by his wife's side,' I retaliated.

'OK, I'll fire him,' she relented. 'He was trimming my firs too tightly.'

'Can't you get the gardener to do that?'

'Oh no, he's too busy with other things', she replied. I think I preferred being the enslaved cupid. There are too many cast members for my liking – she'll never get the costume budget passed by McKinney. Perhaps the gamekeeper's one . He seems to be dressed in very little, when dressed at all.

September 27th – Dr Molly Beaujolais

1 am – had a surreal dream about Dr Jonathan Nylon with him dressed as a butler in the buff style costume. We share a romantic moment in the Tudor Maze, I take off his bow tie and fling it aside. It lands on a protruding sheer, poking out through the hedgerow. Moments later a figure resembling Edward Scissorhands emerges. It is Beacon. He tries to fasten the bow tie onto his neck with his scissor hands but cannot manage it. He cries a single tear, which withers a dandelion growing up through the bracken below.

September 27th – Dr Jonathan Nylon

A good meeting with Professor Lannister today about the progress with the Norwegian Campaign. She is quite an attractive woman actually – American with short straight brown hair. Not attractive like Molly of course – she is like the Moon and Molly is the Sun. I wonder if Molly would be impressed with that Shakespearean reference? I couldn't tell her though, don't want her thinking I'm lusting after every woman in the department! Professor Lannister has a penchant for oversized Aztec-looking jewellery. Her arm looks like an internal column at Trump Tower. She probably has the missing Blenheim Palace toilet (all gold) stowed away in her office. I don't understand

women's fashion sometimes. Unless Molly's wearing it, then it makes perfect sense. She looks good, as my sister's 'Dream Phone' used to say in a camp East

Coast American accent, 'whatever (s)he wears'.

Lannister is a bit concerned that I have strayed too far from my topic. 'It's a bit combat heavy Johnny,' she said. 'A literal blow-by-blow account.' She's right, I have become obsessed with the battles, maybe obsessed is too strong a word – preoccupied. I reconstructed Eskimo (complete with bow) out of the sauce pots yesterday. And I've been having some vengeful thoughts about annihilating Kyle with a Vickers 1913 BL 6-inch Mark XII naval gun at close range. I was thinking of using Eskimo as a paper weight in my office, but I don't want to distress my students any more. They're already on the brink by the sounds of it. I had one call me up the other day saying he was feeling suicidal! One of the few on my 'Medieval Ailments, Medicines, Crime and Punishment 'module. Lectures haven't even started yet! I think I need to change the title, grouping it all together like that might cause confusion – and anxiety clearly!

4 pm – just bumped into Dr Peacock in the Tudor Maze, and she told me through a hole in the patchy leaves that Molly is dating some East End hunk called Beacon who writes poetry. I hope the spirit of Shakespeare was also listening in and will intervene for this lovelorn Benedict.

September 28th – Dr Jonathan Nylon

I consulted Molly about my outmoded modules today and she suggested I inject some modern life into my syllabus. Apparently, there is a course at the University of Westminster called 'Pop Goes the Now' which is all about cross-referencing various epochs in history with our own. She pointed me in the direction of some new wave websites that will keep me up to date with pop culture. The first image from a site she showed me on her phone popped up in more ways than one! A bizarre looking gentleman with a ghostly look of Boo Radley exhibiting his engorged penis for the benefit of another misassembled media mogul. I'm not sure what purpose this article is serving. If I wanted to see the unsightly manhood of a skinny white man, I would look down (there would be less logistics involved) or at Mr McKinney, whose face bears a striking resemblance to the wizened scrotum of an old Cornish pirate.

The story goes that he has been sending these saucy snapshots to all and sundry, and people on the internet are not happy. I understand the premise, but what I don't understand is who they are, and where did they come from – as Cilla Black would say, 'Where do they stand on the great conveyor belt of world history?' What are my students and I supposed to learn from them?

What can we learn from ...? I can't remember their names, they're all bizarre animal or superhero-related pseudonyms. Is that too simple a question for third years? I'm really struggling to cater for this term's students' needs. Where are they heading? Where is history heading with 'vloggers' at the helm? Where am I heading? For an iceberg.

I should've kept my job at the meat factory and stayed in beautiful Bristol – Julie Bainbridge didn't care where we all stood on the conveyor belt of history, or conveyor belts of any description – only that mutton chops fell off them and paid for her New Look handbags.

I tried to dig out some more intel on my rival Beacon, the poet laureate in waiting, but she seemed to want to talk about teeth for some reason. You never know which way the conversation will turn; I'm learning to roll with it. She told me a story about a dentist called Jacopo she dated in Milan who rang his finger along her teeth and said, *'tuo sorriso non è perfetto'*. Then she smiled slowly and revealed the perfectly imperfect set in question. The vlogger should consult Molly in the art of subtle seduction – I could feel my face aflame like hot summer tarmac, like the scorched earth of Bloomsbury Square! I panicked and for some unbeknownst reason shoved my hand in my mouth and displayed my own ghastly gnashers – then grinned like a village idiot. She seemed quite pleased by the whole charade. Maybe she likes goofy characters. I'll have to show her my Brouwer postcards.

2 am – have thought about Molly all day and now I am thinking about her all night. Captain Per Askim cannot compete. He'll have to wait (again). It seems Beaujolais is going to be as much of a distraction as a woman as she was as a man!

September 28th – Dr Molly Beaujolais

Beacon has gone on a Jack the Ripper walking tour of London. I need space. I should've tipped the tour guide to lead him on a merry dance, like a miscreant taxi driver. I fear that the Ripper's death count isn't high enough to keep him at bay for as long as I would like.

I knocked on Dr Johnny's door today, with a couple of teas. I think I am trying to seduce him.

I can't wait to see his crooked smile and hear his quirky history-laden anecdotes. He was trying to talk to me about making improvements to his syllabus,

I ended up showing him some obscene photos of vloggers. I'm not interested in these unattractive people or improving his students' minds; I only want to make him blush. Oh God, I don't belong in academia. I belong in an asylum – perhaps an upmarket one for retired artists, like in that film *Quartet*. I want to touch his eyes and his teeth. He showed me the ones at the back today. I hope he hasn't cottoned on to my secret passion for them! I was telling him the tale of Jacopo, then he put his hand in his mouth and exposed his misshapen molars. I had to look away for a moment.

Two more days until Beacon leaves. He has very white teeth, but they are as straight as Bedlam's bars.

September 29th – Dr Jonathan Nylon

I've purchased the coffee machine and gramophone (out of my own modest funds) – I can't be waiting for an audience with Mr Brown every time I want to make a decision. It was making me feel emasculated.

Molly and I went for a bagel and cup of tea at our little record cafe. We still haven't made any progress with the quiz; we are enjoying each other's company too much. Lessons in pop culture continued: a singer called Sam Smith wants to be called 'them'.

People are not going to remember to do that. I remember trying to get people to call me Johnny at school, they still kept calling me Pantyhose.

'Well, they should try to remember and respect their wishes,' Molly said. 'People have had a complex relationship with gender for eons, Johnny, it's not a new thing. Many simply do not feel called to either, it's always existed, but now we're giving it a name.'

'So, he keeps his name?' I said.

'Yes, they keep their name.'

'So he wants to be referred to as them not him ... as in the Royal We?'

'As in they're non-binary,' she explained.

'Ternary,' I said.

'Look, it's not an us and them scenario,' a customer intruded ... clearly it is!

When we left, I said goodbye to the cafe assistant (I think he's the manager) to make it look like we're friends and keep up the charade that I'm cool. He's the only one over 25, he has grey hair and horn-rimmed spectacles, not that that's an indication of age these days! I said, 'I like your nails, what colour are they?' 'Shellac.' I don't think that's a colour, but I could be wrong! He then turned to Molly, with a slightly dismissive air and enquired after 'the buff Bloomsbury set bae' who was 'on her arm the other day'. She has been coming here with the East End man! I feel betrayed. The shellacked figure then blurted out that this 'Beacon' had made up a poem in "the heat of the moment". I was having a heated moment of my own, in one of Dante's seven circles of hell!

12 am – looked up the Sam Smith story, don't want Molly thinking I'm gender intolerant. There was a very helpful article on the Guardian website with a pop out box explaining what a pronoun is.

September 29th – Dr Molly Beaujolais

Beacon and I tried out a romantic gesture this morning, but it backfired horribly, like a homemade firework display. I was writing up some book ideas in bed, not getting very far. Beacon asked what I was doing – I said writing him a poem, he asked me to write it on him – somewhere he can see it, like his shoulder (the first warning sign there – the Catherine wheel spinning at a sub-standard rate!). I wrote the words in the shape of a lighthouse, to commemorate his namesake. He managed to get a look at it eventually, after a bit of manoeuvring, like a dog chasing its tail, but the sentiment was lost on him. He said, 'It's very detailed, but you've missed off the left ball, the right one is a bit wonky and all.' The right one being a craggy rock. I wish I hadn't spent so long on the trailing flora along the coastal path. He has no sense for what is artistic and true. The man is a monster! Frankenstein's monster. He is lost! He needs to be lost, *Paradise Lost,* in that cave with Milton and Dickens and emerge literate. Even then I couldn't guarantee he wouldn't meet a similar fate to the monster and be shunned by society at large. Not even David Copperfield's magic can save him now!

After we kissed goodbye, he tenderly traced the Pink Cascade on his temporarily tattooed shoulder with the tips of his fingers and then the line of my cheek bone and said, 'Next time I come back, I'll take you to Paris.' I have judged him too harshly – he's not the brightest bulb on the Christmas tree, but he is a sweet man. I am full of remorse.

8 pm – just got back from Pilates with Luce. There was one lone man there in a sea of warrior posing women. 'Must be a pervert,' she announced as soon as she

spotted him. I think he heard, he looked very uncomfortable shuffling from upright cobra into downward dog. She told me about how she tried to go for a walk in Battersea Park earlier and had ended up crawling through bushes and onto a highway with no barrier. She should've called Beacon for assistance, he seems to have spent most of his life surrounded by more bushes than people – the early days in particular when he was cast out, naked, from the doctor's laboratory into the big wide world must have been spent largely hiding in them. We shared our woeful dating stories – I told her about Beacon and Tybalt. But kept back my secret desire for Dr N. It was a relief to get into child's pose.

1 am – had a dream about Dr Nylon and Beacon. I was dressed in a white lab coat and was assisting Dr Nylon in a lobotomy operation – Beacon lay on the table in his best Lacoste pants, surrounded by a full auditorium of students and staff. Professor Veal let off a firework, which spiralled its way to Beacon and singed his beautiful hair. I fell upon Dr Nylon in

floods of tears, which caused his hand to slip, and he removed the entire frontal cortex.

September 30th – Dr Jonathan Nylon

I have been in a bitter rage all day. My mind is wracked with jealousy about this metrosexual Beacon character. There is another one called Mercutio or something, who is trying to worm his way into her affections as well – I hope she makes worms' meat of him.

I went for a stroll to recalibrate my humours and chanced across the allotment dwellers – tenderly turning over potatoes with their grotesquely calloused hands. I bent down to tie up my shoelace, in preparation to move on, but as I stood up, my face came in contact with one of the grizzled hands, which had suddenly appeared over the fence in my absence. It was like that shower scene in *Psycho*, with less nudity (praise the Lord!). 'Hi ho,' a voice called out. Before I could respond, an elderly man of about four foot in stature had made his way around the fence and was hobbling towards me with great haste, like Old Rumpelstiltskin at a haberdashery sale. He was wearing a gilet garment in a carpet-like fabric, which looked like it had been fashioned by Julie Andrews for one of the less fashion-conscious children.

I shared one cup of Darjeeling with the man (with a far from moist Garibaldi supplied by another minuscule character called Margot) and admired his amply proportioned turnips and now I am a fully signed up member! The Labour party should take a leaf out of Leslie Jumbo's tea caddy. He is a very persuasive man. I doubt he's ever experienced woman troubles.

Wrote a poem for Molly when I got home:

Your mind is like a greenhouse,

I can see right inside and there are rare and exotic flowers

And beautiful ripe peaches waiting to be fondled and plucked (but only handled with love, care and attention and when the timing is right, or they are in the mood)

... And there is also a grotesque looking apple scrumper, who has been warned to stay off the land, but keeps coming back like an apple bobber gasping for air – gawping through the glass at the precious fruits and there's a bicycle inside next to them, propped carelessly against the wall that everyone in the village is trying to have a go on.

I think it needs tweaking. Maybe I'll come back to it once the shadow of Beacon has blown over, it's dampening my poetic sensitivities. How can I compete with this Mike Tyson/Benedict Cumberbatch character?! Brains, brawn, and a poetic soul! My soul is as haggard and dry as Margot's baked goods.

September 30th – Dr Molly Beaujolais

Oh God! A terrible thing has happened. I was drinking in my office (I don't need to pretend I was working to you, dear Diary). I heard some kind of strange crackly sounds coming from Dr Nylon's office. I crept out and put my ear to the door and suddenly Edith Piaf came blaring out, belting *'je ne regrette rien'* at a deafening volume! I jumped out of my skin and the wine glass leapt from my hand! It was very dark – where the heck is the light switch?! I hope it didn't leave a mark.

September 30th – Dr Jonathan Nylon

I've made a few purchases at the record/bagel cafe:

1 x smoked salmon, cream cheese, rocket and capers bagel

1 x tea with milk

1 x 7", 45 RPM Vinyl Single – Muddy Waters*, Rock Me / Got My Mojo Working*

1 x 12", 45 RPM, Vinyl Single – The Clash, *I Fought the Law*

1 x 7", 45 RPM – Edith Piaf, *Je Ne Regrette Rien, Les Mots D'Amour, Jérusalem* (B side) – I'm not a fan of this one, just bought it to impress Molly – she's writing a book on forgotten French artists apparently – she was a bit vague on the finer details.

Spent a large portion of the afternoon just looking at them displayed on my desk, whilst drinking macchiatos. I'm not going to know what's hit me once lectures start!

10 pm – I've just seen Molly disappearing down the stairs in the dark at breakneck speed, I opened my door a fraction and she was gone! I'd made a couple of macchiatos for us; she has been working late like me lately. I was thinking I might try out my poem on her (just the first line maybe). Perhaps she was fleeing from McKinney, he was coming down the hall from the opposite direction. It is hard to get out of a conversation with him once he gets going, especially

with Scottish independence becoming a hot topic again.

I wanted to show her the new gramophone, I hope she's not going off me already!

October 1st – Dr Molly Beaujolais

I've seen the door and it is terrible. Avoided Johnny all day. I can't face him; he will be devastated. He has quite a materialistic streak.

October 1st – Dr Jonathan Nylon

Je regrette tout!! I am in shock! Came in this morning to find a garish red stain emblazoned on my door! It begins at the door handle and finishes at the frame of a print of *Sunflowers*, on the wall next to it, tapering off into a zigzag, like the mark of Zorro. Vincent must be turning in his Auvers-sur-Oise grave.

So that's what she was up to, scuffling about my door last night – carrying out a cruel act of vandalism! She hasn't said a word about it either. It must be her – the students avoid me at all costs and McKinney is strictly a whisky man. It will be macchiatos for one from here on in.

October 2nd – Dr Molly Beaujolais

Got cornered in the corridor by McKinney today, he pinned me to the panelling with his steely blues. He wants me to take on the role of piano accompanist for the staff choir. He said it was his late wife's dying wish that he continued to use his singing voice for the good of others. What was he using it for previously – sadistic purposes?! I think he knows about the red wine and is punishing me. It will be an ordeal if he is joining. His speaking voice has a very nasal tone, I can't imagine him sending a wee bairn off to sleep with it – killing his wife, perhaps. It could cut through a 90-piece symphonic orchestra, complete with Wagner tubas.

Rehearsals are on Tuesday evenings.

October 3rd – Dr Jonathan Nylon

The suicidal student is a hypochondriac with PTSD from being left alone in an NHS hospital bed for several hours while his limbs swelled up with blood. I don't think the 'Medieval Ailments, Medicines, Crime and Punishment' module is for him. The first lecture was on leeches and other superstitious medical practices. He did well to get through it, he made no notes, but sat bolt upright for the duration and looked very wide-eyed. Unlike some of his classmates – who looked like they'd had a heavy dose of opium and hemlock. One was in such a deep sleep that his head pivoted back and forth on his neck like an uptilted pendulum. Slumped so far down on his chair as to be virtually horizontal, he resembled a rubber glove reclining on a wash basin (two objects I doubt he's ever had much contact with). The fictional Mr Muscle may have more actual muscle tissue.

      I need to do something to enthuse my students.

I haven't seen Molly since Monday and even then, it was just the back of her head, which is not enough.

October 4th – Dr Jonathan Nylon

Climate change protesters lost control of a hose loaded with fake blood yesterday. The doors of Whitehall have been painted red. I'm not usually one to sympathise with apathetic MPs, but today is an exception. I've tried scrubbing my door with a host of different cleaning products and nothing will shift the stain! Branded for life. My students will think I'm a homicidal maniac and then if they're brave enough to ask if I am or not, I'll have to tell them it's red wine, which will lead them to believe I'm an alcoholic. So far no one has come a knocking – so we'll cross that bloody bridge when we come to it.

October 4th – Dr Molly Beaujolais

I think I'm going to start my students off with monologues – that way I only have to deal with them one at a time.

I miss Johnny. I can't see his face (and teeth) from the distance we keep. Well, I can, see the teeth that is, they're plainly visible at 200 yards – but it's not the same.

October 5th – Dr Jonathan Nylon

George has been asked to put together a feature on 'The Happy Club' (a scheme designed to support disadvantaged and isolated residents by providing household supplies and other objects) at Jaywick Sands. He turned up with Demelza. He said the interview went well, but Demelza cramming items from the tables into her H&M bucket bag in the background was a bit distracting. 'It was like a planned robbery Johnny,' he said. 'I kept him talking while she loaded the shit. For fuck's sake. Oh Johnny, I was hoping to cover Beatrice and Edoardo Mapelli Mozzi next year.'

He's never getting an invite to that wedding. Not if Demelza is his plus one. She'd have cleaned out the entire pile of gifts by the first toast.

October 6th – Dr Molly Beaujolais

How come in Jane Austen books (and their ITV adaptations) the women seem to get rich, eligible blokes to flock to them by being indignant about coupling off with the boring, ugly ones. I've had that attitude all my life and it's never done me any favours.

Just watching *Sanditon.* She should choose the sturdy Gloucestershire one – but the issue is (as it always seems to be in period dramas) she can't overcome the niggling notion that he might be a bit thick. Why are the West Country ones always cast as simpletons? Johnny would not like that – his people being misrepresented. He is very sensitive about being perceived as intelligent.

Beacon has no such sensibilities – even so I'll have to watch *Sanditon* on catch up when he comes to stay next. I don't want him comparing himself to Sidney Parker.

October 7th – Dr Jonathan Nylon

Bumped into Molly getting a macchiato from the machine this morning (another betrayal). We've just been attempting to draft the quiz. I've had easier afternoons. The first challenge was steering the conversation away from her multiple (it seems) lugubrious affairs and dating horror stories and back to the task at hand. Of course, the whole experience was rendered even more fractious by the fact that she re-decorated my door several nights ago in a style favoured by the Israelites at the time of the ten plagues.

So far, we have:

Which classical composer was a crossdresser? Answer: Saint-Saëns apparently (she claims she can't remember anything else from her music degree).

Even though every loop and line she made with her 2B sketching pencil (she has completely illegible writing, she'll have to read the questions) felt like a compass scouring my heart, I couldn't help but feel a familiar and unwelcome twinge of passion for her. We talked a bit more about her book, she says she's taking a surrealist approach to it, in the manner of the founders of 'l'objet trouvé' – opening pages of reference books at random and sticking in quotes. I said, what sort of quotes. She said: 'Is the sky green?'

'Ah, as in, is the pope not in any way a pervert ... sorry, first thing that came into my head, he actually seems like a very nice man. As in, classically abstract ones?' I rambled.

She said, 'As in, I don't care.'

She is a true anarchist. She seems to come from a long line of them. Apparently, her family live in a house formerly occupied by the last man in London to be hanged. If she thinks I'll be impressed by such an association, being a history lecturer – she's mistaken! She said it with such relish – clearly, she thinks the criminal life is one of glamour and proprietorial stability.

It took a good twenty minutes before we had some words on the page. We certainly have vastly differing work ethics. I am fancying my chances more and more by the day, however – after hearing about the charity worker, who left a woman for dead in her penthouse apartment on the first date and the one who made her pick a card every time they had sex to determine the position (aka the current record holder for the longest game of Solitaire). Then there was the theatre producer who told her all her stories are 'race-led'. I can see where he's coming from, they do all start with: 'this [insert nationality] man'. I reassured her by saying 'if anything it shows you are a strong advocate of multiculturalism.'

Despite their blatant flaws, it was still an agonising experience listening to her reminisce about her past loves. Although I didn't take much in, I was too busy watching her lips and thinking about kissing her. When I stood behind her in the queue to check out our library books, I had a strong urge to pull her pigtails. 'Hitler Strikes North' had left a red rivet along the palm of my hand afterwards, like a Hegra Fortress trench, where I'd been gripping onto it. All my expeditionary forces had headed south.

October 8th – Dr Molly Beaujolais

My obsession with Dr J and his distinguished teeth continues. You could drive a toothpick between each one, but never a wedge between our hearts? Disaster! He doesn't seem to be impressed by my admirers, they are a bit of a motley crew these days – all court jesters and penny stinkards! I hear him playing his records like Carey Mulligan in *An Education* and I long for his attention. How can I get it? Anne Boleyn threw an orange at Henry VIII's head to get his.

I think perhaps he would prefer a soothing citrus balm applied to the temples. He seems a bit stressed at the moment. We were standing outside his office door today and he kept widening his eyes and raising his eyebrows in a peculiar fashion – maybe it's the quiz. He was very agitated by our library session yesterday (we are struggling to come up with material). I'm afraid he'll vanish once our work is done – I think

I'm trying to delay the proceedings. I don't like this new professional slant our relationship has taken on.

8 pm – first 'choir' rehearsal concluded. The choir is just **Mr McKinney** so far, or Alec as I've been invited to call him now. I accompanied him in a soul crunching rendition of *Will Ye Go Lassie Go* to an audience of his dead wife's ghost and then he let this lassie go. Thank God!

11 pm – I've written a poem for Johnny:

Your eyes had a look, blurred

As if there was no one clear emotion in them

The oil painted dot, dipped against the water's edge

Rippling out into the room

But I can't hear the rest

Just your rest

And your hand, resting in mine

October 8th – Dr Jonathan Nylon

Molly made me a cup of tea this evening in a mug featuring Lionel Richie's face with the words, 'Hello, is it tea you're looking for?' She was holding two bottles of London Pride in the other hand. She said she was in desperate need of one, after a choir rehearsal with Mr McKinney. Blimey – what 'rough magic' is this, I never know what's going on at this university! I was grateful for the tea, but only drank the beer. When she offered it to me, we had a painful exchange where I had hold of the blisteringly hot mug's main body and she had hold of the handle. Rather than letting go and saving me a third-degree burn, she proceeded to warn me, 'it's hot, be careful' – to which I replied, 'thanks, yes.' After a couple of cycles of this call and response, she finally twigged and let go. The hot liquid offering had what looked like a dusting of chocolate sprinkles on top – a bit unusual, one of her little jests maybe. Probably just 'tea oil' as they say, or dust. I caught a glimpse of her office the other day – she is very messy.

I tried to give her a look with a nod to the door that said, 'I know you did it, but I forgive you and

94

adore you', but I couldn't get her to hold my gaze for long, she was fixated by the door. Perhaps she is finally realising the magnitude of her transgression. When I turned to go back into my office, I put my scalded hand on the cool handle, and she put her hand on top of mine. The cold beer bottle sent a shiver down my spine. I'm not sure if it was a mistake – we still can't find the light switch. I hope not.

I was so flustered I forgot to return the mug afterwards – and to drink the scurfy tea. I can still feel the impression. She has left an indelible mark.

October 9th – Dr Molly Beaujolais

I want my students to be creative, but re-inventing themselves as a cartoon version of a fight (those ones with a cloud of dust and legs sticking out at odd angles) is taking the piss. Today is Actors' Day, acting class number one. I opened the door to a scene from Mad Max set to a soundtrack composed by Lionel Bart and Kander and Ebb. There was no way I was going to break up the musical, theatrical- wrestling extravaganza unfolding before my eyes with my presence alone. The long-haired Liszt character at the piano was in stage animal mode and could not be stopped. In a bid to regain/gain some authority, I deposited the scripts with some force on top of the piano. I meant the gesture to inspire respect alla Deloris in *Sister Act*. In reality, it inspired the piano lid to close on his fingers. Less Goldberg, more GBH.

Florence Chambers kicked off the proceedings with an overtly passionate reading of Jill's speech about homeless people in *Radiant Vermin*. I don't think she's a regular *Big Issue* buyer somehow. It was a relief when the next student got up.

'I'm standing before you this morning with a troubled heart,' he began.

'A very troubled heart,' I interjected. I thought I better make some contribution.

'No,' he said. 'My Nan died this morning.'

I wanted to make a joke about not being footloose and fancy free and reconnect with the students after the violent start but thought better of it.

When the next student got up and started reciting Othello's 'I have a weapon' speech, I let it slide, just in case. He definitely has Othello's menacing character down.

The final act was a comedy duo.

Robert Galloway had chosen *Macbeth* Act II, scene i monologue: 'Go bid thy mistress when my drink is ready'. For some strange reason Dido Clark got up with him.

'Why are you standing up?' I asked him.

'I'm playing the part of the servant,' he said.

'The servant doesn't have any lines in this scene,' I said. He explained that he hadn't had time to prepare.

I explained to him that the servant characters are often thought of as the most outspoken in dramaturgy and typically represent the voice of the masses, in the hope of instilling the lie that by choosing to play the servant he will have more lines to learn. But he was insistent – servant roles suit him best. The Dido had been cast.

He is going to go away and have a look at the part of the slave in *Waiting for Godot*. It's like the Peasants' Revolt never happened.

October 10th – Dr Jonathan Nylon

Bursting for a pee all the way through my lecture today. If I'm not careful I'll develop a blocked bladder, like some of these poor medieval folk. Not brought on by venereal disease in my case though. A chance would be a fine thing! The students were in a very jovial mood today, they particularly enjoyed the description of a medieval kidney stone operation:

'The patient sits on a man's lap . . . the physician stands before the patient, inserts two fingers into the anus, pressing with his left fist over pubes.'

When I was collecting up the student's debris at the end, I spotted a very detailed sketch of the procedure, featuring a character that looked alarmingly like me! The rest was not accurate. I will have to include more anatomical notes (maybe an appendix type handout with diagrams) next time.

Spent all morning trying to find Molly, she wasn't anywhere on campus, it was highly irritating – the quiz is tonight, and we still have no real material. Caught McKinney eyeing up the red wine stain in the hall as well; my sanity is on its last dregs.

1 pm – I have drafted some questions in between meetings and my book writing schedule. They'll have to do!

October 10th – Dr Molly Beaujolais

No lectures today.

Spent the day in bed with Beacon the beautiful boxer – we are in love/lust again now we've had some time apart without conversation. He surprised me, turning up unannounced with a bunch of wildflowers and a copy of David Copperfield's *Master of Illusion* DVD (remastered from the 1984 VHS). Had an irate call from Johnny at 2 pm, mid lovemaking. I don't think I've ever heard an angry Bristolian before (although he doesn't really have the accent, just the yokel rambling style of talking). He opened with a list of nonsensical questions without saying hello. I managed to butt in at Jesus of Nazareth. He's cobbled some questions together; they're an unusual mix, a bit on the dour side to be honest – but I can't be arsed to write them, so that's fine. He made me lean over Beacon's perfectly formed torso and grab a pen and paper to write them down. This is what we have so far:

Who is this? (Picture of Adrien Brouwer)

Which alcoholic beverage was forbidden due to its excessive consumption in court by Chanakya in India, fourth century BCE? Bonus points for the specific type of said beverage.

Answer: wine (madhu)

What colour was the door of Number 10 Downing Street during the fruitful year of 1908, before it was coated in irremovable black emulsion?

Answer: Green.

Why did Jesus of Nazareth die on the cross circa 30–33 AD?

Answer: He was betrayed.

How many years did John Herbert Dillinger spend in Indiana Reformatory and Indiana State Prison?

Answer: Nine.

What was his mother Mary Ellen Lancaster also known as?

Answer: Mollie.

How did Cummings, Dillinger and Frechette escape from the scene at the Lincoln Court Apartments shoot-out in 1934?

'I think we've got too many about this guy, Johnny. I've never even heard of him!'

'Answer: down the stairs and out the back door. And as a bonus question: Why did the police turn up? Answer: They were betrayed (by Cummings).'

And the last one is: which composer was a cross-dresser? Answer: Saint-Saëns (my humble contribution).

'Just need to double check this one,' he said. 'Do you think that's enough?'

'I think people will be ready to dance by then, or hang themselves, yes.'

'Oh, what about this , I thought we could put this in – a question about your address and the last executed man?'

'I already have a student who's said his desired career path is 'to find a route into my knickers'. I don't think leaving an Easter egg trail of clues to my front door would be wise.' That made him laugh. My desired career path is to make Johnny laugh.

5 pm – came into the kitchen after our conversation had finished (and I'd finished writing it all down) and Beacon was waiting there wearing only a pair of oven gloves and holding a cold whole roast chicken with all the trimmings. We'd been over an hour on the phone, and we've also scheduled an 'emergency meeting' (in half an hour) to hone our material. A blazing row ensued. Not sure how I'm going to get that roast potato down from the curtain pole without his help. I agree it is unnecessary to meet so early when Johnny's already written the questions. I tried to explain that there is plenty more to discuss – how to divide the delivery of questions, who will add up the points etc. But it is becoming harder and harder to deny my obsession with Johnny – when I am not talking to him, I am talking about him. Beacon and I, however, had run out

of things to say by this point and ate in uncomfortable silence – our roast chicken without the trimmings.

The lights have gone down on our love affair. He left before pudding. Osiris be praised.

Our boy, Beacon, has the body, but he doesn't have the words. Or the teeth.

October 11th – Dr Jonathan Nylon

I danced with Molly last night. It was one of those cinematic, coming-of-age Steve Barstow/school disco style moments when the music changes from fast to slow. Ironically, the track was *Don't Let Me Down* by The Beatles because that is exactly what I did. It was the best five minutes of my life, followed by the worst five hours. She was close enough for me to kiss her and all I could think about was Beacon the Boxer. I asked her for an exact rendition of his limerick – she looked at me with her beautiful hazel eyes and recited the most exquisitely simple and touching poem I think I've ever heard. No wonder she fell in love with him! I should've told her the truth, but I was too jealous to give it its full credit, so I gave it a firm but fair critique instead. Anyway, I ballsed it all up. She looked very unimpressed and turned away – into the arms of some suave artistic types. I felt a bit sorry for Beacon actually! It takes a lot to win this woman's heart!

The quiz was a relative success – well, certainly in comparison to the rest of the evening. Well attended. Molly had invited two of her friends, Bobby and Luce. They were actually one of the few groups to get more than two questions right. One of which was the one about Jesus Christ. Well, they put 'fucking Judas', but I gave them a point.

Luce kept hers and Bobby's answers well hidden in a toxic cloud of cinnamon-flavoured vapour. Bobby took on a look of (a more jaded) Johnny Depp in his Sauvage advert – engulfed in a plume of exhaust fumes. They are deeply strange people and Molly's closest friends. An artist and a composer, from her 'fin-de-siècle' set no doubt – end of the road more like! Bobby looked like he'd been driving around Route 66 on a loop all nigh – the bags under his eyes were like the shadows of two flying saucers in amongst an unruly wheat crop. I don't think the man's ever felt the intimate caress of a Gillette blade. Apparently, he's felt the intimate caress of both Molly and Luce though (his other teammate), Luce was telling me later in the evening. This revelation rubbed more salt in the wound but paled in comparison to witnessing a similar scene actually playing out in front of my eyes.

Molly spent the remainder of the evening with the two artistic tools that had whisked her away from me on the dance floor: scenic painters studying at the Slade, apparently – my informant Luce told me. The whole second half of the night was taken up with them all salsaing to the likes of *P.I.M.P* by 50 Cent and *The Bad Touch* by the Bloodhound Gang. Bruce Forsyth would turn in his grave. One got her plastered and the other one gave her a rough cast finish. It was torture watching the Chuckle Brothers passing her between them like a bit of flimsy plywood.

She left with Barry. Or was it Paul? They're all the same these artists.

October 11th – Dr Molly Beaujolais

I want Johnny, but he thinks I'm a fool! He said, 'My poem 'isn't exactly *The Lady of Shallot'* (why are all his references medieval – he must have a penchant for revenge and retribution). I recited the whole thing to him, while he held me in his arms – then he said, 'It's good, but not a limerick,' and the rest. Anyway, I met a couple of scenic painters from the Slade: Coburn Gold and Vincent De Boussay. Vincent wanted to go home with me, but I turned him down in the McDonald's queue, I hope we parted on good terms, the last thing I said to him was 'parting is such sweet sorrow, now fuck off.' I wanted to impress him with a highbrow literary reference, but my lowborn status won out.

He says he has a fascination for all things beautiful, like my shoes – he asked me to take them off so he could inspect them fully. I hope he appreciated me risking catching a cocktail of diseases from the nugget-laden floor. I gave him the left one; it has a nail sticking out of the inside near the heel –

better give him the warts and all perspective from the off. He can only ingest beauty he said, refusing a chip, everything else his mind rejects. I'm surprised he stuck about so long with Luce talking about her IBS in such minute detail, I saw his beautiful full eyelashes squeezed into a wince on several occasions. 'I can't imagine her getting in a mess,' she said, nodding in the direction of a pristinely turned-out twenty-something woman standing coyly with one of those boyfriends who wear boat shoes that I can never get.

'Just do it on the floor,' a punter called out.

'Someone already has I think.' Vincent looked accusingly at me.

'A lady never tells,' I quipped.

11 pm – Vincent has added me as a friend on Facebook.

October 12th – Dr Jonathan Nylon

Spent all day at the allotment. I tried to leave after an hour, but Eunice coerced me into raking over her cabbage patch. Their wrinkly smiles may give the impression they are benign spirits, but they're slave drivers, the lot of them! Anyhow, it was a welcome distraction from ruminating over the disastrous events of Thursday evening. There is always some peace to be found there, nestled in the locally supplied clods of soil and odd bits of broken glass. The quality is not up to Haskins standards. I was struggling to get my turnips properly turned and a large Polish man called Iwo gave me a few tips. The simple act of kindness made my eyes a bit moist, unlike the soil, which is as dry as one of Margot's homemade Garibaldis.

I also had a nice chat with Leslie Jumbo. He may look like a harmless old gent in a polka dot neckerchief, but he has a colourful past – a very colourful past indeed. He took me through his tattoos one by one, each one has multiple stories to tell. Terry Clarke brought some homemade jerk chicken pasties, which were amazing – I feel like I'm in the boys' club. Eunice, Margot and the other ladies were tending to the plum tomatoes. We ploughed the land and reminisced about old times – their times were older than mine, so some of the conversation went a bit over my head. I'm surprised a person can still feel so passionately about the changing shape of a three-penny bit – but then again look at the uproar the reduced size of Freddos ignited. They've invited me to the social on Friday – for committee members only (so now I'm a member of the committee – news to me!). Eunice made me take out my diary and write it in on the spot, she really has me under her thumb. So, it is literally in the calendar! Dear God. I'll have to cancel drinks with Dr Jacobs.

October 13th – Dr Molly Beaujolais

Checked in with Joleen, the Goar affair is still raging on! Well raging is an exaggeration, limping stoically forth, like a speared Spanish bull. Goar has sent a smouldering selfie in an attempt to rekindle his senorita's wavering flame. The image was taken in a low-lit room, with Goar laid out on a traditional

Spanish rug, by a hearth – various knick-knacks surround him. 'His forehead is so low, Molls, it's practically resting on his eyelids! I can't do it anymore.'

'Maybe he was trying to be expressive,' I said.

'Cubist, more like,' she said. He said, in Spanish: 'Every lined crease is the bill of how ardently I desire you.' Google Translate has become a third wheel in their relationship she said – another bone of contention. 'They are signs of premature ageing and stress, babes,' she replied, in bastardised Spanish. He's invited her out to Spain for his aunt's 80th fiesta celebration. 'When's that?' I asked. 'Five years' time,' she said. Oh God, he's in it for the long haul. The long-haul flight at least.

8.30 pm – watching *Sanditon*. Where is the romance in my own life? I think I'm going to delete all these dating apps. A man I've never met just asked me if I would like to have his head between my legs, I think I'd like to see it at eye level first! A luxury Goar will never experience. His furrowed brow will not permit a level gaze.

October 14th – Dr Jonathan Nylon

First lecture on Narvik today, but I couldn't get my head into it – with Molly going round it. I feel like an empty husk. *Eskimo* de-bowed. I need to tell her how I feel, it's all getting a bit Petrarch and Laura. I really should start showcasing these literary references to her – this one could backfire though, our man Petrarch was of a slightly obsessive bent – I don't want her bolting off again, like a thoroughbred fleeing the stable. She would run for sure eventually, she is too good for me. She is Black Beauty destined for great things and I am Peggy with the short legs, who hardly has any lines, or Old Oliver who gets killed in one of the first scenes. The scenic painter is Ginger no doubt, all that biting she does – I can imagine he'd have an aggressive, perverse streak. Doesn't bear thinking about. I'd like to think I could make a comeback as Justice later on, repairing the damage that Ginger has raffishly inflicted. Whatever I do, I need to stop making analogies to *Black Beauty* – if Molly ever found out about my extensive knowledge of Anna Sewell's classic, she wouldn't want to set foot in the same yard, let alone mount me and ride off into the sunset.

5 pm – found another peculiar etching post lecture. This time it was a sketch of two battle ships colliding – one with love hearts firing out of the armament. I hope they were playing a game. My face had been superimposed onto the front of the mast of the one with the love hearts, like a Thomas the Tank Engine character. I've been trying to wrack my brain to remember who was sitting there, but they all leave so quickly afterwards, it's hard to recall.

October 15th – Dr Molly Beaujolais

Introduced my students to the improv game Park Bench today, which we've paraphrased as Tube Seat to make it more relatable. Apparently, it's weird for people to sit on a park bench for an extended period of time these days. 'The Cat', Andrew Lloyd Weber's falling meteorite, juvenile Deuteronomy, the Cat who got the cream (and all the best biscuits) insisted on doing a very ostentatious warm up for such a stationary exercise, the reason for which was not clear. All was revealed however (in more ways than one) when his turn was up. Florence and her Chelsea-mum-of-two inspired character were not impressed with the routine and pulled the emergency stop, leaving him alone straddling the plastic seat.

It was just me and Dido left again at the end of the class. Dido remained sat still in the 'tube' seat for some time. I asked him what he was doing there, and he said: 'just enjoying the moment ... it's nice to get a seat on the tube.' He is a very odd boy. Always outstaying his welcome in someone else's scene or in reality. I asked him how Lucky is coming along. He had no idea what I was talking about. He is one of my favourites.

9 pm – a few more recruits at choir rehearsal this evening – Sandra and the maths lecturer, Cudjoe Jacobs. We're having a crack at songs from the shows. McKinney has a compilation book. He did *Nowadays* with Sandra and now I can't get the image of him in a white feather boa out of my head.

When the choristers had cleared out, he probed me on my book. There was something about his intense gaze that made it impossible to tell the truth. As far as Alec McKinney is now concerned, my book is on a Basingstoke born dramatist called Nathaniel Bucket, who relocated to Paris in the year of 1895 to join the fin-de-siècle artists. He enjoyed a glittering career at the time, but his works have fallen into obscurity since – like a lost Dorito down the back of the sofa. 'For you were made from dust, and to dust you will return'. (He was also a fairly religious man in his youth.)

1 am – message from Vincent: 'How's the lady? And more importantly, how are her shoes? Did they survive the night bus steps and walk home? Did you survive the night bus, or did you need to use the nail to defend yourself?'

1.01 am – message from me: 'They survived, but it was touch and go for me the next day – and the bus driver, when he tried to drop us off five stops early.'

1.37 am – Message from Vincent: 'Glad to hear it.'

1. 45 am – Message from Vincent: 'I would very much like to see them again. And you can come too, if you like.'

Then I sent him a short video clip of my feet in the battered, old red patent Mary Jane stilettos, cross-legged, my left foot bobbing up and down a bit, with the message: 'They're nodding.'

Oh God, what am I getting myself into. What will be next, a re-enactment of Jack and Kate's car love-making scene with sock puppets?

October 16th – Dr Jonathan Nylon

Started reading *Black Beauty* again. It's been a while since I allowed myself to indulge in a bit of reading for pleasure. Molly told me last week that she had given Beacon a reading list. She should put more effort into her syllabus – I had one of her students wander in here the other day who seemed to be confused about what course he was studying and where he was frankly! I seized the opportunity to try out the cappuccino setting on my coffee machine and find out how things are going (she's seemed a bit out of sorts lately). After three double shot lattes, he really opened up. In a metaphorical sense, although I personally wouldn't be able to contain such a generous amount of caffeine in one sitting. He didn't stick about long (he sloshed a bit of latte on the floor in his haste to get out in fact! Good God) and looked a tad uneasy during the inquest – might've just been the plastic chairs they've introduced. He was really singing Molly's praises despite his evident discomfort and confusion. She inspires wonder and perplexment in every man she meets!

5 pm – McKinney has just come and knocked on my door – I was hesitant to let him over the threshold, like a vampire. He caught me mid-reading session – I had just reached Chapter 4, 'Getting Used to Things'. I was at the line about being 'frequently ridden'. I had to put the book down after reading the words and compose myself – my heart and everything else still aches for her. McKinney's arrival was an unwelcome interruption – things were just beginning to look up for Beauty. She finds a seemingly safe haven at Birtwick

Park in this chapter, if my memory serves me correctly. Well, you should never get used to things here, because disaster is always just round the corner.

The time had finally come.

I opened the door a crack, so as not to reveal the coffee machine and gramophone and also to prevent him from disintegrating under the bright light of my Anglepoise. He pointed to the door and widened his eyes – his eyebrows were straining to escape his critically crinkled forehead and his nostrils were flared like Ginger ready to strike. I gaped like a coy carp that can no doubt be found in one of Birtwick's many ponds accessible to the public.

'Was it you?'

'No,' I answered.

'A student?'

Again, 'no' was my response.

'Then who?' he said.

I contemplated offering a variation of 'who stole the cookie from the cookie jar?' in order to keep the terse talk in a secure loop, but he cut in:

'Does it begin with **M** for ... Molly,' he purred menacingly in his ballsy **B**ally bray. I let out a strange ambiguous sound. I'm not sure what you would call it, but my heart knew what it was – the sound of ultimate betrayal. 'You'll be receiving a letter,' he growled. A letter – **M** for Murder no doubt. Certainly not one signed **M** for Molly. She would never speak to me again if she knew.

11 pm – still in my office. The latte has left a stain on the floor. Oh Christ. Oh Molly. I can't stop looking at it, it has sent me into a hypnotic trance. I can hear the janitor's keys jingling as he walks down the hall, the word 'traitor' resounds around my chamber with every trochaic step. He wants to lock up, but I'm glued to the spot. Now I know how Sir William de la Pole felt. The executioner's blade would be a welcome reprieve.

October 17th – Dr Molly Beaujolais

Students failed to turn up to class today – they have joined the 'Extinction Rebellion'. Dido stumbled through the door with a tub of PVA glue, asking where the others were. He hadn't got the memo about the meeting place; his expression was an exact replica of curtain-haired Kevin's when he turned up in full school uniform for the Year 7 school trip to the Science Museum. No amount of stationary purchases in the gift shop could assuage his pain. Dido was planning to take a stand against climate change by securing himself to a South Bank bench with a thick coating of polyvinyl acetate – at least he's picked a cultural hotspot, perhaps he will learn something by osmosis. He won't stay put long – he is positively allergic to culture.

October 18th – Dr Jonathan Nylon

Received two very curious letters today. The first was slipped under my office door. An abnormally courteous missive from McKinney, requesting I visit him in his office at 4 pm today. The other was left on my desk post lecture. At first glance, I thought it was a bank statement that had escaped from my satchel. It looked very official, in one of those plastic envelopes with my name printed in a formal/bold Helvetica type. You can imagine my horror then, dear Diary, when I opened it to find a pair of ladies' tights inside and the note:

A pair of nylons for my Nylon

Perhaps one day we could wear them,

Together

I hope they aren't suggesting we take a leg each, like in one of those joint onesie type things. I wouldn't fancy getting in one of those with Grace Kelly, let alone this salacious student character.

Thankfully this one was unillustrated. I have a very photographic memory. Dreading meeting

McKinney later, I've suffered enough emotional trauma for one day.

5.30 pm – life is nothing but unpredictable. Mr McKinney has just asked me if I would be interested in dating his cousin! Her name is Wendy, and she is a tar barrelling champion from Ottery St Mary. I don't even know the man's first name, why would I want to get intimately acquainted with his kin?! Let alone one who partakes in medieval torture rituals. Perhaps he thinks we will have a connection. I need to stop telling that 'Why was the Jester almost executed? Because the Queen got the joke at the last minute' joke. Clearly, I'm setting myself up for the grand execution of the love life of my dreams. My heart is hung, drawn and dodecasected as it is. We've never ventured past formal niceties such as the weather and Donald Trump's latest blunders before – McKinney and I that is. I hope this Wendy and I will never speak – it was a real curveball. And a very unwelcome one at that – she must be at least 60 years old! I think he sensed my reluctance because he mumbled something about *Strictly Come Dancing* being on. 'Oh, now?' I heartily exclaimed. I thought that might have been my ticket out of there! But no. 'No, Saturday nights . . . it's not the same on catch up,' he trailed off. How can I refuse him, he knows Molly is to blame for the red wine! He has my balls over a barrel, a keg of flaming tar to be precise!

I saw Dr Jacobs at the vending machine and broke the news to him about next Friday. I asked him if he's ever seen Mr McKinney's cousin before. He said he bumped into her at the Dominion Theatre, she was talking to Mr McKinney, dressed in a steward's uniform – she has just started working weekend evening shifts there. He said she looks like a poorly put together Mrs Potato Head, although he's just had twins, so his references are bound to be child related. I'm choosing to be optimistic. I looked glumly at a bag of Tayto crisps clinging to the metal ring and mourned my fate.

October 18th – Dr Molly Beaujolais

A man in red and yellow lace-up shoes left a *Metro* and half a sandwich on the seat for me on the tube this morning. Boris Johnson is up to his old tricks again – the classic electric shock handshake joke judging by the open-mouthed expression of Jean-Claude Juncker on the front page. Well, it won't be a shock when the country falls apart, we've been well prepared for that. I turned the page to get the details of the finalised Brexit deal and smiled weakly at the woman opposite me who was applying her lipstick, she returned the gesture. Unfortunately, her real smile was then obscured as the train jolted, causing her to decorate her face with a red joker style grin. The words 'send in the clowns' flashed through my mind. I must have mouthed the words or otherwise it was a moment of unexplained telepathy owing to the current zeitgeist, because the man next to me leaned over my shoulder – looked at the paper then raised his eyebrow in the direction of the woman and said, 'Don't bother, they're here.'

October 19th – Dr Jonathan Nylon

Met my sister in town today. What is going on at Farringdon station these days? Are TFL exclusively hiring failed actors or something – every announcement was like a bloody audition for the RSC! I want to know when my train's getting in, not hear Caliban waxing lyrical. I took her to a trendy cafe called Prufrock's coffee shop. I tried to make a joke with the barista by asking if I could have my life measured out in tablespoons, by life I meant sugar. I don't think she appreciated it, she told me I can pour my own in. I asked Jess how little niece Tilly is getting on. She said she picked up my graduation picture the other day and carried it around the room for 20 minutes before setting it down next to a toy giraffe and a scouring brush with googly eyes and dried spaghetti hair; they were having a tea party. Everyone is welcome at Tilly's table. Meeting her made me feel very homesick and nostalgic.

When she left, I nipped into a bookshop and purchased the prequel to *Black Beauty, Black Beauty's Early Days in the Meadow.* She caught me on the way out, however – she got to Farringdon, but the announcements were pissing her off so much she decided to go home via another route. The shame of being caught clutching the equine novella was akin to the time she walked in on me masturbating into my football sock. Nobody knew which way to look.

12.30 am – I've just had an irate call from Mr McKinney saying Wendy has been waiting for half an hour in the rain for me to collect her. My weary head had just hit the pillow and the next second his name lit up my phone with an angry buzz – it's like he knew!

He won't be happy 'til I'm resting in my grave that man. Firstly, why didn't she wait inside?! And secondly, why do I have to collect her? It's 12.30 am! I thought he wanted me to take her out on a date – everywhere respectable will be closed by now. 'From the theatre,' he explained. 'She finishes at midnight.' Apparently, I am supposed to drop her at 7.30 pm and collect her at 12 am, what am I supposed to do in between, watch her work or drive around picking up other poor lonely women of London from their night shifts – a benign spirit trawling the city streets, a phantom coach driver more like – I'll be bloody knackered, usually in bed by 11!

It all adds up now – I did wonder why he kept mentioning the over-inflated prices of black cabs during our chat the other day. What would Molly think of me if she knew I was being pimped out like this. I once dreamed of being a racing car driver. Look at me now. I'm providing a taxi and escort service to a passive-aggressive, posh Scot's aged cousin.

October 19th – Dr Molly Beaujolais

Vincent rang to say he's taking me to Margate. 'To see the Turner Exhibition,' he elaborated. We've been texting nonstop since Tuesday. I now have a visual catalogue of my entire shoe collection, should I need it.

10 pm – we've arrived in Margate and are staying at the Sherwood Hotel. Vincent likes it because it has net curtains – he's never seen them in real life before, he

said in his lilting Dylan Thomas legato, peering out of them at the sea view.

'We can watch the tide blinking at us, while we're bleary-eyed and winking at the world. '

I'm not sure what that means, but I hope he's not going to be winking at the whole world, he's already been flirting with the receptionist – suggesting we get another set of keys cut for her. I let it slide. Made a cup of tea with the little kettle (one of life's greatest joys!) and enjoyed the view – Vincent.

October 20th – Dr Jonathan Nylon

Margot offered to read my palm at the allotment today in exchange for a vine of my tomatoes. I am now freely throwing myself onto Charon's boat to spend time with the ungrateful half dead. When I showed a bit of reluctance she said, 'They ain't worth the soil that put them there.' After examining my hand, she said she couldn't make out any of the lines because it was too smooth and underworked. I tell you, Diary, underworked it is not – they've got me doing the lion's share of manual labour! Worn down from years of abject loneliness, potentially. I think she might have been punishing me because I withheld my ripe tomatoes from her. Then she told me that she'd been to see that one from *Strictly Come Dancing* in *Big the Musical* and it was a wank. Well, I wasn't handing over my Tumbling Toms for that mystic revelation, I could've told her that for free! I decided not to pick up my usual jojoba oil hand cream on my way home. Don't want women thinking I'm not the rugged, manly type.

Spoke to George on the phone. He is texting a man on Grindr who works for the Department for Exiting the European Union.

'I have to keep Googling what he's saying Johnny. If we go out on a date, I'll be glued to my phone all night. He's clever – do you think he's too clever for me?'

Well, he must be clever if he's working on Brexit. 'No, course not,' I said, 'he's probably just used to talking in impossible riddles.' Talking of impossible riddles – when I got home, I discovered a pair of beige 'old ladies' knickers in the washing machine with my laundry. What sorcery is this?! I'm not going to that allotment anymore.

October 20th – Dr Molly Beaujolais

Set off early to "beat the queues"– I think Vincent has an exaggerated perception of the popularity of the Turner Gallery in Margate, we were the first ones there. The wind was wild. It whipped my hair into my face and the faces of several passers-by. I couldn't eat my Mr Whippy ice cream, I had to just let it melt into my hands and the furry cuff of my tobacco-coloured teddy coat. I must have looked like Medusa on a seaside break from the underworld. Apparently, I looked like an altogether different character, an altogether very different character from most. 'You remind me of Turner,' Vincent turned to me and said.

Turner was an uncouth Cockney who didn't fit into artistic society. 'In this light,' he added. Does he actually think I look like him, or is it one of his playful jests? I would say he's no oil painting, but that would be a lie. He is the Mona Lisa of men. Perhaps I should start wearing old man's tweeds. Whatever poisoned breadcrumbs he throws me I can't help but consume body and soul – he is wickedly handsome and intelligent.

The first exhibit we chanced upon was entitled *Walled Unwalled*. It takes a look at how secret information is attained through walls and doors, but we didn't go in. I had a look while Vincent hung back, standing behind me in the corridor. He said he had a better view from where he was. He then changed his mind and poked his head through a crack in the door – he is a bit of a voyeur.

I enjoyed Helen Cammock's one: 'Histories are never behind us ... They are part of who we are, who I am, who you are.' I can't ever think about making work that's about contemporary life that doesn't involve histories. Must remember to tell Johnny, he'd like that.

I wasn't too sure about Tai Shani's piece. 'I don't like this one, makes me think of umbilical cords – I'm very squeamish,' I said. 'Oh, that's a shame,' said Vincent with a manic glint in his eye.

After that we went to get another ice cream and I had to hobble across the stony beach in my heels, like a lobster trotting on its claws. We gave up halfway and Vincent threatened to throw them into the sea. We kissed with our feet in the sea – and our hearts in the clouds.

October 21st – Dr Jonathan Nylon

My office smelled like porridge this morning (prison). Goes with the whiff of stale coffee and guilt. The medieval people would christen it 'a foul air' and would expect an epidemic imminently. There has been an awful bug going round the university. The latte stain has got bigger, it cannot be covered by my size 10

Oxford brogues. Although I'm not one hundred per cent, I don't like standing on it for long because it reminds me of a sinkhole. My conscience cowers under the shadow it casts. Metaphorical shadow – there's no actual shadow now the foam has evaporated. I think it must have carried on leaking out into the grooves of the floorboards over the weekend. Or I'm going mad. One of those possibilities is a dead cert.

I thought I'd make the lecture a bit interactive today, so I got the students to group together in tens to teach them about the medieval justice system of tithing. I think I will stick to a more formulaic approach in future, some students did not take the exercise seriously. One member of the posse comitatus asked me if I had ever been in contempt of court myself, to which I replied 'no'. He then added in an undertone 'for being a bad boy'. Is he the one? The knight in black satin sheen tights! I'm choosing to ignore it and hope it will run its course. I wish someone would run this course for me, these medieval folk are making me suicidal now. I was reading about the array of medieval punishments on offer in Whole Foods the other day (not on offer in Whole Foods – that would be a shock for the puritanical Americans that frequent it!). I was reading about said punishments (involving every element, for every crime under the sun) and had a sudden urge to ask the man sitting next to me to stab me with his wooden fork! Thankfully, it passed as quickly as it bobbed up. Unlike the poor convict in the case study – who passed slowly, never to be seen again!

October 22nd – Dr Molly Beaujolais

8 pm – here endeth the choir rehearsal. The new recruits have not returned. Alec and I tried out a few Irish ballads this evening and some English ones; I've never seen him so amenable. He would like to stage a concert, I'm not sure how to break it to him that he's not ready – and never will be. His interest in Nathaniel Bucket has been piqued. He was hungry for specifics. I spun him a yarn about his escapades in Paris – days spent cruising the boulevards and nights spent sketching prostitutes.

'Ey? He sounds like a right pervert?'

'Cruising for poetic inspiration,' I said.

'Oh aye. And did he find inspiration?'

'He did.'

'Aye, I bet he did. What was she called then?'

'She was called Aubrey.'

'Ey? That's an old ladies' name.'

'Well, he wasn't discriminate.'

'I see, all for the art, ey. Nathaniel you dirty bastard. And what did she inspire?'

God he's persistent. 'A play.'

'What was that called then, I'll have to look it up.' He won't do that, he can't be bothered to look up the page number in his *Book of Ballads,* he always peers over my shoulder.

'*Night Vowel.*' I said

'What's it about?'

'It's about the moon.'

'Oh aye, a full moon, eeey?'

(*The Golden Glove* had put him in a lascivious mood.)

'It's about a man from New Jersey who sees a vowel emblazoned on the moon one night.'

'What is it, an O?'

'No, something more distinguishable?'

'What do you mean – are you asking me?'

'No, that's what the man thinks, out loud, in the play. He's asking the moon for it, the man from New Jersey.'

'Oh aye, what's his name?'

'He doesn't have a name. He's just referred to as 'the man from New Jersey'.'

'Well, it's one way of filling up his word count. Who's calling him that?'

'No one.'

'Oh aye, talking about himself, is he?'

'Yes.'

'Oh, carry on.'

'He sees an O, but he's looking for something more?'

'So, he hasn't seen a vowel at all?'

'Perhaps, perhaps not. It's a magic surrealist, post ... end of, fin, fin-de-siècle. Very Dada, darling.'

'Very gaga.'

'Aren't they all?'

'These Basingstoke born 'French' surrealists.' I don't know why he emphasised the French like that, I never said he was French, only a European at heart.

October 23rd – Dr Jonathan Nylon

Bumped into Molly this afternoon, literally, as I was stepping out the door with my head down – trying to avoid treading on the latte stain, I think for superstitious reasons.

Standing with Van Gogh's sunflowers behind her, she was like a single red rose in a bank of stumpy sedums – the Guinevere to my King Arthur, the Vicks to my Prince Albert, the heady vapour from my beloved coffee machine, the rubber to my royal seal. I think I'm coming down with a cold. I need to ask her out soon. If I've caught what Branston has, I may not have long to live. I found him the other day, draped over the men's sink, coughing like a bastard! He needs to cut down on the canteen Friday fish and chips. I had to escort him out like a drunk girl in a club.

I wonder what Molly would wear to a club? She was wearing gingham checked capri pants and a white woollen jumper today. I know what 'capri pants' are because I bought something from Gap once, and now they send me regular stock updates. I wanted to scoop her up like a lamb and carry her away – not roughly slung over my shoulder though, like the shepherd in our family nativity set. And not far, I don't know if I have the upper body strength (neither did the plastic shepherd – Spike, our Jack Russell, snapped him in two like a brittle twig one Christmas) – just into my office, or somewhere safe and warm (so definitely not my office then). God, she's so lovely.

7 pm – plucked up the courage to ask Molly out, but that bloody artist bloke has beaten me to it and some bit on the side called Mr Fordy Man! Another bloke in her harem! Her manopoly of admirers. "A typical cocker" he is apparently, "always on the go". Not in Bristol they're not, they're usually slumped over a park bench by 2 pm. Must be all that hearty East End fare – keeps the old men going. I can't stand the thought of this Mr Fordy Man's jellied eels coming in contact with her perfect placket-lace. She is not a sheep; she is a wolf in sheep's clothing – more than capable of finding her own greener pasture or a herd to devour – a herd of stags! Any shepherd with pure intentions is cast aside like a homemade jumper at Christmas time. She has quite unravelled me. I asked her if she wanted to

go and see the Turner Prize exhibition in Margate, I thought we could laugh at the weird ones, but she said she's already been to see it with Vincent . She invited me to come and see his exhibition next week, she said we can get fish and chips afterwards and pretend we're in Margate. Pass me the wooden fork.

October 23rd – Dr Molly Beaujolais

Johnny's been very odd lately – he's really getting on my wick actually. We were just discussing weekend plans and then he got all pissed off and started going on about 'me too' for some reason, how men don't like to be used and abused and cast aside either – so I left him to it. First, he slags off my poem and now he's taking umbrage with Mr Fordy Man! He avoids me all week and then this. He's probably one of those people who don't like dogs – homicidal maniacs. Sandra told me he's going out with Mr McKinney's cousin as well – what the hell's all that about?!

October 24th – Dr Jonathan Nylon

Kyle is having a Halloween party next Sunday and I have been told I will have to vacate the house. I go of my own free will Kyle! I should've gone for that elderly house share/housekeeper living arrangement, with the reduced rent. I would have crippling back pain and no social life, but at least I would be happy. I'm going to drive home again, once I've deposited Wendy, she'll have to make her own way home – we are not joined at the hip.

Kyle requested I pick up some fava beans for him – he wants to try out a recipe for the party. It was a very embarrassing experience. I tried Whole Foods first, I wandered the aisles for twenty minutes, but couldn't't locate them. Couldn't bring myself to ask the attractive shop assistant for them either, I'd come straight from a lecture and was carrying a student's medieval torture textbook, left behind on the desk again. I wasn't about to add to the creepy serial killer look I was already so successfully showcasing. The book was left by the hypochondriac student – he's not going to acquire anything from the book for Christ's sake! A disease or anything else for that matter – certainly not a lucrative career in the outside world. I refused the delicious looking miniature brownie she was offering, nervously shaking my head like a maniac. I eventually found some pre-prepared salted fava beans, I had to get down on my hands and knees to read the fancy writing. The attractive shop assistant gave me a curious look when I stood up again – she was probably thinking 'Buffalo Bill' has finally cracked, and he now thinks he is actually a buffalo.

When I got to the queue it was 30-foot-long and being held up by a man with a trolley full of goods in a silver NASA bomber jacket – genuine merchandise apparently. Genuinely awful more like. The shop assistant said, 'I love it, you could fly to the moon in that.' I think the woman behind him would've liked to have put a rocket up his arse to get him there. I sent Kyle a picture of the purchase, but they were the wrong thing, he needed raw ones – and my raw nerves cradled in his narcissistic hands. I traipsed round three more supermarkets. Again, I couldn't face reaching out to the shop assistant for help – these fava beans were becoming a sort of private addiction I needed to keep concealed from the world. I considered saying

they're for a friend, but that sounded even worse! By

the time I got to Lidl, I was in such a heightened state of anxiety, I was brought to the brink of a panic attack two steps from the entrance – it is very disorganised in there, like a bring-and- buy sale. I walked straight out again – patting my pockets before leaving, like Dick Van Dyke doing his chimney sweep dance number, a

charade intended to convey I'd forgotten my wallet. In

the end I bought him some butter beans from Tesco – he will have to learn to face the fact that life is full of disappointments, I've put my sanity on the line for these beans. He owes me a nice bottle of Cabernet Sauvignon for my troubles, or Chianti – I'm partial to both.

October 24th – Dr Molly Beaujolais

Vincent and I discussed our wedding today, so I'm going to delete the apps. A text from Tybalt during dinner: 'I want to see your bare bum before I die.' It was hard to deny a dying man his last wish, but necessary. The last man to crop up luckily was Atlas from Cheshire, who said he would like to take me to a remote island via a helicopter to drink hot chocolate and marshmallows until and during the sunset. Easier to turn down that one – I wouldn't like that, having no means of escape, although at least he'd put a definite time limit on it. Vincent said he could fall in love with me and he's going to tell his parents about me.

I said, 'What have I done?'

He said, 'There's no one like you, but then again there's no one like anyone – look at that bald man over there, he's someone's special someone.' At the words the bald man raised his head from his plate of pasta alla Genovese, as if Vincent had just heralded her arrival.

Our views on the wedding are not congruent. I would like to have Balulalow from Britten's *Ceremony of Carols* as I walk down the aisle. With little lanterns falling like snow and wildflowers tied to the pews, to make it look like an edited scene from *A Midsummer Night's Dream*. The after party (reception) band would be a lively gaggle of characters called The Mechanics – they'd play 'Come on Eileen' on Baroque strings and 'Bob the Builder' from *Can we Fix It* for the kids. 'It sounds beautiful,' chimed in the bald man. I suggested we could drag the Loughborough bell ringers out of retirement to attempt an extent on eight bells, complete with all 40, 320 permutations. There are a lot of people in my family, I explained and many elderly ones, it will take them a while to climb the church path. I thought about 12 bells, but the sequence would take over 30 years. I looked at Vincent in his 90s vintage Ralph Lauren jumper, looking over my shoulder at the waitress. Perhaps the 12 bells would be more appropriate.

We listened to St Paul's choir singing 'Balulalow' on my phone in the restaurant.

'It's very eerie Molly,' he said. 'The vicar won't know whether we're making wedding vows or a suicide pact.'

'Either/or,' I said, 'he'll be a priest. We don't have the same distinctions in the Catholic Church.'

He said he would wear tartan, even though he's not Scottish, because he looks good in green. He couldn't get away with a kilt, he has very spindly legs. I didn't say this at the time though. I didn't want to spoil the moment. The final piece of the ensemble would be a white fur coat. I'm not sure how I'd feel advancing down the cold church tiles towards a piece of cotton wool perched atop two pipe cleaners. Although the music would be beautiful and the lanterns landing on him would look like glow-worms collecting on a snow-covered hillock. Or we would look like Beauty and the Beast about to tie the knot, and I don't wish to emulate a Disney themed ceremony alla Katie Price and Peter Andre.

October 25th – Dr Jonathan Nylon

12 am – have just returned from the social with the oldies. God, again what would Molly think if she knew I was spending my Friday night hanging out with these crumbling crematorium dwellers? Is there any aspect of my life I don't wish to keep secret from her? I'm struggling to think of one!

Branding Bingo as a 'leisure' activity is very misleading! As scribe, I spent the entire evening in a heightened state of acute stress. I've never been so relieved to see a tray of roast potatoes, brought out by the barmaid at 'half-time' and generously distributed to the frenzied throng. It is not a game for the fainthearted and arthritic. I'm surprised so many old people take it up! You've really got to have your wits about you – it tests the reflexes of every sinew and fibre of the body and brain. A moment's hesitation could cost you the game and your life, if you're playing with Margot. I couldn't manage a fourth round; I was out for the count at the end of the first! Thank God for the 11 pm curfew and the local convenience shop's inability to attain a licence to sell alcohol – Terry and the gang would never have let me go otherwise!

October 26th – Dr Molly Beaujolais

Vincent has invited me to a Halloween thing next Sunday (one of his arty Goldsmiths/Central Saint Martins friends). Gosh, I was looking forward to an evening in front of the *Strictly* results show in my slippers. Now I'm going to have to don some four-inch heels and dance the dance of the seven veils until sunset!

October 27th – Dr Jonathan Nylon

I'm writing this from the comfort of my old bedroom, in the beautiful Waterley Bottom. I say comfort, there is condensation on the inside of the window. I've been helping Dad prepare the tups and rams for market this morning, in between copious cups of tea and charred homemade flapjacks. A group of decrepit hikers strolled by earlier – I offered them one of the cakes. One turned to the friend, bypassing me and dad and asked, 'what is it?'

'They call it a flapjack,' replied the other one. We call it burnt offerings in these parts, but each to their own. I think Molly would love it here, she'd fit right in, with her sheep jumper. I think about her all the time now, in between practical musings and medieval-themed suicidal thoughts.

I need to think about her, although it pains me, to distract me from the horror of my 'date' with Wendy. She makes Mrs Potato Head look like Brigitte

149

Bardot! Molly makes Brigitte Bardot look like Mrs Potato Head.

Thankfully Wendy was able to make her own way there on this occasion. It took me a good half an hour to locate her at the theatre for collection. I had actually come across her in the first five minutes – but with her back turned, facing the corner, I had mistaken her for a man urinating. It soon became apparent, however, that she was just taking a sip from a flask of tea "with a wee nip of something extra", to keep her going. Apparently, they're not allowed to drink on shift – she was going at it a long time, I'm surprised she didn't get caught. She wiped her mouth like a lusty peasant at Henry VIII's wedding banquet and tucked the flask into her steward's belt.

She is not as old as I supposed, maybe mid-40s. Ms McKinney has not aged well! Her hair is like a block of Wensleydale cheese. It's actually more the colour of Cornish Yarg, I'm not sure why I wrote Wensleydale – I think it's because she reminds me of the female farmer from *Wallace and Gromit*, which is not altogether bad. She was a childhood favourite, although not a teenage pin-up of mine. I nipped to the toilet, for something to do, and when I returned, she had undone one of her waistcoat buttons. It's unfair to say she looks like a Mrs Potato Head, she has very clearly visible human female attributes.

She invited me to sit opposite her on the 'steward's seat', situated at either end of the entrance to the stalls like his and her thrones, while we enjoyed the final moments of *Big the Musical.* She told me the title several times, emphasising the word 'big' – she must think I'm hard of hearing. When we got to the song with the words 'the piece that was missing was one special man', she mouthed the lyrics to me and held my gaze. Perhaps I imagined it, it was very dark inside, but I think she also mimed a sort of scooping gesture aimed at my heart. I hope she's not planning on harvesting my pound of flesh! The moment was soon interrupted as Shylock turned her attention to an unsuspecting young man, who had been filming the entire second half. He must have felt the hot glare of her gaze, as he swivelled around in his seat with an alarmed expression. She gave him the old two fingers to the eyes 'I'm watching you' gesture and that was the end of it – he dropped his phone in a panic. 'I'm not paying for that,' she muttered. Like brother, like cousin.

October 28th – Dr Molly Beaujolais

I'm worried that I'm attracted to gay men. I keep seeing them from afar and falling in lust and then another man strolls up and takes their hand and my dreams away. I'm afraid that Vincent will turn out to be gay. Although he's given me absolutely zero evidence to prove that theory so far. I asked him how often he thinks about sex with a woman the other day and he looked at me quizzically and said, 'As often as I can.'

Came across an article in *The Stage* from last year that claims we are set to lose 40 million pounds in arts funding because of Brexit. Nothing more on the subject since (no follow up article). No one has commented I guess – too busy enjoying the plethora of cultural activities currently on offer to them. My students will have to be off book then – since books will be off the stock supply menu along with everything else. I've been trying to think of a suitable play for them to perform. I've had a few unsuitable suggestions from the students. We need something for a cast of 15. The Cat has written a new English libretto for a full-scale production of *The Tales of Hoffmann* – all characters are robots made from low grade aluminium, to reflect the synthetic and ultimately ephemeral nature of existence. There are multiple references to Kleinsack's sack. Well, he's cocked up there –

Kleinsack is clearly a living, heavy breathing man. With all the necessaries to prolong his temporary existence through procreation at that!

October 29th – Dr Jonathan Nylon

No lectures today – thank God. I've been up since 4 am though – thinking about Molly. Considered catching up on *Bake Off*, but I've missed every episode but the first one, where the one with the man bun went out. Probably for the best that, it would have divided the nation and our sceptred isle is fragmented enough. Also, I find the harsh critiques and self-loathing difficult to stomach, all these poor domestic types damning themselves to hell for a soggy bottom and Paul Hollywood cackling manically as they go down in flames. It's not what it used to be, when it was in the loving, dough-soft hands of the BBC.

Watched *House Doctor* instead, swiftly followed by *House Busters* with a cup of tea, not very imaginative programming there. Paranormal activity is causing anxiety for a family in South London, I think, still – I'm not sure if things were ever resolved. It was fairly painful viewing, partly down to the presenting, but also because I was sat on a knitting needle for a large portion of it. Luckily the needle was attached to some handiwork (so I don't need to sleep with one eye open) – a large crochet blanket to be exact, featuring a 180° aspect of St Petersburg's Palace Square. It was a very detailed and skilfully executed piece of craftsmanship actually. Kyle has gone up in my estimation as an artist, if not as a human being.

Went for a long walk on Blackheath, there was a fine mist about, like angels' breath. It made me feel like I wanted to go sit in a church. I popped into the one in the middle of the heath and immediately wanted to walk out. Strangely enough, Terry Clarke was sat with his head bowed in one of the pews. A choir rehearsal was about to start, and the vicar eyed me with a wild look of desperation disguised as affability. I understood why once the choir started. When the descant kicked in, Terry said, 'Sounds like someone falling off a cliff,' in his smooth Jamaican accent. It's very early to be singing Christmas carols, but I suppose they need the practice. We sat and talked for a bit – well, I stage whispered and Terry talked at full volume, despite the glares from the altos. I told him all about Molly, the stain scenarios and my manic military/sauce pot episode. He said, 'We're all mad Johnny boy, look at Margot – she has a head shaped like a haricot bean.' I don't think the shape of Margot's head has a direct influence on her mental state, unless you're going by Johann Caspar Lavater's theory of physiognomy. I thought the church had moved on since then. Apparently not, if they had, surely the vicar would have given the good-looking tenor more of a hard time, he'd missed every entry from what I could make out. Pleb. He looked a bit like Vincent actually, the posh one from *Made in Chelsea*. I mentioned that to Molly the other day, but she didn't appreciate the comparison.

October 30th – Dr Molly Beaujolais

Sandra and Cudjoe have returned to choir, but I can't see them coming back for more after last night's debacle. Alec tried his hand at conducting and it turns out he has a firm one. We are attempting to learn an ensemble number, the 'Lacrimosa' from Mozart's *Requiem*. I don't know about the deceased in heaven, but I was weeping inside. Every time anyone made a mistake, he made them return to the beginning of the work. It was like a tortuous game of snakes and ladders played with an unyielding and bad-tempered grandfather.

I tried to sneak off at the end, but he cornered me. Firstly, to play and sing the tenor solo in the 'Tuba

Mirum' (the part his wife used to sing). Then when my eyes started flickering to the exit sign, he set off on Nathaniel Bucket again – I have opened a can of worms here!

'I – erm – looked up Nathaniel Bucket, but there were no results on Google. What was the name of that play again?'

'*Night Vowel.*'

'Oh aye. Has he written anything else?'

No, no he hasn't Alec. Because he's made up. He's a complete fiction.

'What has he written?'

'He's most renowned for a devised piece called *The Sound of Parlance* – it's a lyrical work about how people speak when they think no one's listening.'

'Who?'

'People who use a certain parlance, people with jobs.'

'What sort of jobs?'

'Like stagehands.'

'Stagehands from 19th-century fin-de-siècle theatres?'

Yes! Why does he keep questioning that? Is it so improbable that a boy from Basingstoke visited Paris a hundred odd years ago?! I think he has lived a very closeted life in Braemar.

'Yes, his use of the contemporary vernacular is very striking actually.'

'Ah right, what's the first line then?'

'Well, there is no first line.'

'There has to be a first line.'

'It doesn't come until the second act.'

'Fucking hell. What happens in the first act?'

'It's a setting of the scene, one man is lying on the stage and another one is up a ladder.'

'These are the stagehands.'

'Yep.'

'So, no talking at all, ay, and how long does it go on for?'

'Forty-five minutes.'

'Fucking hell, forty-five minutes with no fucking talking.'

'Yes. He wasn't for everyone ... and the audience were quite rowdy in those days – there is *some* talking.'

'Ah yeh?'

'Just muttering.'

'Ay?'

'Well, the one on the floor ... '

'Aye?'

'He's just fallen off the ladder.'

'Ah right, and he's just lying there, and the other chappie doesn't help him?'

'No.'

'Why's that?'

'It's a metaphor.'

'A metaphor?'

'He knows he'll be next – it's a metaphor for the cyclical and nihilistic nature of life.'

'Why doesn't he get down from the ladder?'

'Health and safety.'

I can't keep this shit up.

October 31st – Dr Jonathan Nylon

Reading and marking. Marking the days I have left in this travail of a life and reading *Black Beauty*. Chapter 27, Ruined and Going Downhill: 'Soon after I left the stable, there was a steeplechase and he determined to ride.' Black Beauty, poor sod, he's only just set his hooves down in the hay and he's got to get back out there – no rest for the wicked. I must be the complete opposite of ruined because I am resting every night alone in my stable, chasing my own steeple. I will spoil, if I am not released soon. I have the sex drive of a wild stallion, but I am confined to the stalls – the theatre stalls. The only outlet for my sexual emotions is Wendy – an androgynous stable boy.

A heated debate about Brexit broke out in my lecture today. The class is divided like the nation, although we all agreed that we are now, for better or worse, set apart from our European neighbours. There was a note left for me afterwards:

They will never accept us, these Europeans.

Lyubyu vsegda,

Your Vronsky

He is very romantic – I think I'm falling for him!!

October 31st – Dr Molly Beaujolais

Went shopping with Vincent today. He wanted to buy an umbrella from James Smith and Sons on New Oxford Street. He couldn't afford any of them, so we got one from across the road instead for five pounds. As soon as we stepped outside the shop, it blew inside out.

An elderly woman with razor sharp cheek bones approached in a faux Burberry head scarf. 'I want to see you wearing that,' he said. I gave him a confused look. 'Wearing only that. Would you let me tie you up?' He whispered urgently, leaning into me.

Unfortunately, a gust of wind propelled him at the same moment towards the woman, and he directed the words into her ear rather than mine. It was a good job we had the broken umbrella to defend ourselves with.

November 1st – Dr Jonathan Nylon

A very strange occurrence at Forest Hill station this morning. The platform was practically deserted – a man in a devil costume had descended onto the tracks and was attempting to light a fire by rubbing a stick against the rails – he had dropped his cigarette. I think this master had had too many margaritas the night before. No one offered him a light. And then, an even stranger thing occurred – a rail worker on the opposite side of the tracks began to crouch down as if he was going to help him – I turned my head for a moment to look at the announcement board and when I turned back, he had vanished from the scene, and a train had pulled into the station. Perhaps I had had a miniature seizure, I have been suffering from insomnia lately and potentially night terrors. I heard Russian voices shouting outside my window last night. I might ask Molly's friend Joleen to smuggle me some morphine. I'm at a very low ebb.

George dragged me out to a Halloween event in Shoreditch last night. The fancy dress theme was 'what you were scared of when you were little'. I came as 'my own death', only because monetary funds prohibited me from going as 'everything'. The costume had definitely dictated the concept – the top hat last worn at my sister's wedding that I luckily found at the back of my wardrobe seconds before leaving was the main component. I was hoping to pass for an undertaker, but people kept mistaking me for Uncle Fester. He doesn't even wear a top hat! And the man is bald as a coot! I have a very full head of hair. I'll have to start eating more vegetables and cut down on the frothy cappuccinos.

Demelza turned up as Michael Gove. I sincerely doubt she was frightened of him as a child – unless he is a family friend. He's only been in office since 2005 and even that's debatable. George rocked up in a full black PVC catsuit, claiming to be 'the darkness'. 'I didn't know you were scared of the dark as a child,' I said. 'No, I'm Justin Hawkins from *The Darkness*,' he said, 'their high-pitched voices terrified me.' I forget how selective he can be about music sometimes and how odd.

Spent far too much of the evening with an excruciatingly boring man in a sheep costume. Judging by his costume and the nature of the conversation I assume he had a childhood phobia of the rural working classes. He might as well have been bleating, he was so posh and drunk all his words had become melded together – it was like he had switched to speaking Italian. He had to keep stopping to cough profusely, when he started off again, he'd ditched the elided Italian vowels and moved into a kind of Mongolian throat singer style of communicating, one that had consumed the lion's share of chewing tobacco at an all-night shaman ceremony. The man was possessed – with the spirit of tedium. He growled to a halt eventually and passed out on top of Demelza's hot pant-clad backside. Something Gove could not pull off. Although they would suit him more than an MP's garb.

November 2nd – Dr Jonathan Nylon

Kyle stopped me as I was on my way out this evening, to check I was leaving. He was dressed as Dr Emmett from *Back to the Future.* Is he planning on going back in time and pinpointing the precise moment he became an absolute bellend I wonder?

November 3rd – Dr Molly Beaujolais

I'm not sure about Vincent's friends. They're the sort of people who wear a baseball cap to a costume party and say they've come as a concept or a person who writes about concepts. I'm not sure I've ever met anyone who's done that. I met a man who didn't wear shoes and went as a yam to a fancy-dress event once at university. That might've been a way of brushing over his over enthusiastic application of fake tan, however.

Vincent's friends are a type of people anyhow, a type I can't relate to – a type who didn't appreciate my handmade RD-D2 ensemble, complete with tinfoil hat. That's my main gripe. It was quite large and took up a lot of space in the bijou flat.

I abandoned it in the hall after 10 minutes and joined Vincent in the kitchen. He was making elaborate cocktails. We got into a discussion about method acting – he invited me to stare at a whisky tumbler for 60 seconds and imagine it was my dead brother's murderer. If I was unconvincing, I had to lick the wall. I said I would do it for 30 seconds. Vincent considered the performance a success, but I'm surprised I managed it. It's hard to imagine my brothers coming off worse in any violent situation – they are the reincarnation of the Kray twins. I didn't mention this to Vincent, I don't want to scare him off. As promised, he licked the cupboard door, then we disappeared behind the bathroom door and made love up against the sink – I've got a mark like the rings of Saturn on my arse now. He fell asleep in the bath and left me wandering the lonely hall for somewhere to rest.

I found a room, but Vincent's friend Kyle said, 'You can't go in there, that's Jonathan's room.'

'Jonathan who?'

'Nylon,' he said. He shrugged and went off to get another drink and I went in – to Johnny's room.

I didn't know he had a passion for model making. There was a strange construction of a ship made out of ketchup pots. Or a passion for beige high-waisted ladies knickers and black satin sheen tights – there were a pair of each on the back of a chair. Either he's making a tentative exploration into the world of cross-dressing, or he has embarked on a passionate love affair with a member of the nearly home and dry, there's a place waiting for me in the sky club.

I know he has a passion for *Star Wars* – and his mug was on the bedside table. I picked it up and it made me cry. It made me think of how he swills the last remnants of his coffee around the cup before downing them like a shot. Which made me think of his clever, gentle country boy hands and flat spatula-like nails. Which made me think of the way he puts his hands in his pockets when he's nervous, puts his head down and peers up at me intensely, like he's batting in rounders. Which made me think of the way he creases up like a little boy when he laughs, literally doubles up and shrugs his shoulders like his body can't contain the laughter or you're about to hit him over the head with a rolled-up newspaper. And then that made me think of the dimple that appears in between his eyebrows when he talks about the North Nibley Steam Rally, or anything he's passionate or angry about; it's difficult to differentiate. He's a combination of both most of the time. I found one of his old t-shirts to wear, one of those 'Fruit of the Loom' ones you have no idea where people buy – they must inherit them.

I slept in his bed. Which made me think of him, all night and through to the morning.

November 4th – Dr Jonathan Nylon

169

Got home this morning to find someone had written *I lube you Mole* on my mirror in red lipstick. God, I hate Kyle and his associates. Examined my reflection through the smeared markings and I'm certainly not looking as rotund as Uncle Fester. If anything, I look positively emaciated! That wrinkle in between my eyebrows is more distinguished than ever.

November 5th – Dr Molly Beaujolais

Just remembered I wrote *I love you* on Johnny's mirror! Think I tried to rub it out though. Oh God.

November 6th – Dr Jonathan Nylon

Lecture on the Battle of Drøbak Sound today.

If Kommandørkaptein Anderssen could cross the Oslofjord and command a three-strong (Krupp 28 cm MRK L/35) torpedo battery after 13 years of retirement, the least my students could do is pick up a pen and make some notes. Not a single note was made. I know because I handed out the pens and paper and collected them afterwards, which made me ten minutes late for a meeting with Prof Lannister.

More heckling, not from the not-so-secret admirer this time. His lewd comment last lecture has incited mutiny in the ranks. This time the retort was in response to a description of the torpedo tunnels, which despite their age could fire up to six torpedoes without reloading and had a further nine reserves, ready and stored.

'He can go all night then, sir,' the heckler called out from the back row. They have so much to learn.

November 7th – Dr Molly Beaujolais

I saw Johnny in the hall, and I could hardly look him in the eye. I had such an explicit dream about him on Sunday I'm surprised my eyes didn't go into temporary paralysis from the REM.

I've put up a notice for the auditions. *'Tis Pity She's a Whore* has 15 characters. It's inappropriate in every other way, but it'll do.

Alec came shuffling down the hall, dragging his leg like Frankenstein's assistant, just as I was fiddling to secure the last bit of Blu Tack.

'Are you OK?' I said.

'Oh aye,' he sighed. The limp went unexplained. Then he produced some paperwork and a copy of a marriage certificate from behind his back.

'You have been busy!'

'Oooh no,' he laughed, then gazed glumly at the ground for a few seconds. 'I think I might've found our man Nathaniel,' he said. 'It looks like he was born in Texas and married to a Welsh woman called Grug Hickney.'

'Are you sure he was a Basingstoke lad?'

How could I disappoint him now?

'That's right, his father was an associate of Robert B. Hawley.' I stole a cursory glance at one of the pieces of paper in his hand. 'He was a close friend and confidant during the Fifty-Fifth Congress, actively involved in uniting the political pluralities under the single thought of equality for all: Populist and Republicans, German immigrants, African American freedmen and white Democrats. Everyone loved him.'

'What a life ay, so how did he get to Basingstoke? Nathaniel, Nathaniel Junior, is it?'

'Yep,' did not suffice. 'Nathaniel,' I continued, 'Junior, relocated to Basingstoke after the force of the 1900 hurricane drove him from his home.'

'Oh my. Like wee Dorothy ay? I thought he was in Paris in 1895,' he said. How can he remember every minute detail of Nathaniel Bucket's fictitious biography after a single hearing, but he can't remember the second time bar in 'She Moves Through the Fair' despite infinite repetitions, having the music in front of him and me calling out 'second time bar' at frequent intervals before its approach?

'He was, he didn't stay long.' Unlike Alec. Who wouldn't know a French exeunt if it shat in his chapeau chinois. 'I mean, he was famous in Paris for a poem he wrote, aged 10,' I said.

'So, he was 15, when he got together with Aubrey – I don't know about that.'

'No, no ...'

'Oh aye, well – I look forward to Tuesday. I've been practicing the 'Lacrimosa'.'

So have I Alec, so have I.

November 8th – Dr Jonathan Nylon

Kyle is having a bonfire party next weekend. It's like Paris Hilton's bloody home away from home here! I can't keep spending weekends at home, I can't keep up with the manual labour.

Molly offered me a 'sweet treat' that resembled a sunburnt tup's testicle today. Vincent's gone off meat, and their love affair is a non-stop Linda McCartney sausage fest apparently. She said, 'Every word that comes out of his mouth is dripping with sexual insinuation.' Well, I saw him in the canteen the other day and his mouth was dripping with hoisin sauce from a duck wrap, so he's been lying about being a vegan. God knows what other baloney he's filling her mind with.

November 8th – Dr Molly Beaujolais

Dido has put his name down to audition for every single part, including the whore/nursemaid, Putana.

Vincent came to visit me at the university today. Sometimes I feel he looks upon my love for him a little bit how I'd imagine Couperin would look upon Ravel's composition *Le Tombeau de Couperin*, had he ever had the opportunity for it to grace his ears: he'd think – 'what the fuck is this? I never asked for this.' I offered him a homemade vegan 'energy ball' this

175

afternoon and those are the words his face was communicating to me. He told me the other day he's a vegan and he'd appreciate it if I stop going to 'That's a Chicken'. He doesn't like the way the guy behind the counter knows my name and gives me free chips – although he didn't mention anything about murdering animals being wrong, so maybe Nando's is still OK.

November 9th – Dr Jonathan Nylon

Guy Fawkes has nothing on Kyle. Tonight's fireworks night shindig revealed the most elaborate plot of intrigue and betrayal since Robert Catesby sat down in the Duck and Drake with his mates, stared deep into his pint of mead and decided he could see the faint outline of King James of Scotland's death mask in the dribblings of unfermented sugar.

I told Kyle we should invest in some more upmarket fireworks, but he insisted that people make their own fireworks all the time and his weed dealer was an expert. For once I am siding with the Brexiteers – never trust the 'experts'. One rocket was lit. It headed directly for the shed like a homing pigeon on a suicide mission. The wooden structure immediately lit up in flames and from its entrance emerged a family of five! An elderly woman, what I assume are the mother and father and two small children. The elderly woman was clutching a crocheted blanket of St Petersburg and was wearing a traditional Russian style head scarf. I thought at first it might be a hallucination brought on by the weed coated packaging the fireworks had been presented in, but no – they were flesh and blood – still, thank God.

Kyle made a beeline to get inside and out the door. I had to consult the poor traumatised shed dwellers for the full story. It turns out Kyle has been renting our shed for a small fortune, well the same price as my own rent and has been paying £25.60 a month and 'the bills'. I can't believe it. I called the landlord on the spot and gave him notice. I gave the family a cup of tea each and a packet of weed between them. I think they'll need it tonight. We lit a joint off the Catherine wheel and forgot our troubles for a while.

November 11th – Dr Molly Beaujolais

I've just found Johnny crying in the corridor. I've invited him to live with me.

November 11th – Dr Jonathan Nylon

I broke down in my lecture today after a student threw a paper aeroplane at my head whilst I was regaling how 2600 German sailors had joined the ailing ranks during the land phase of the battles of Narvik. I had to leave out the detail that 290 had dressed as healthcare workers and crossed over from Sweden, the only moment of levity in the whole two-hour lecture. They heap misery on their own heads. Molly found me snivelling outside my office. I pretended it was about what happened with Kyle and the stowaways, but really it was because I'd seen her kissing Vincent in the canteen. She gave me a hug, which made me cry even more and my nose ran into her pink, angora cardigan. It was humiliating. I made an abrupt 'ah' sound to try and extricate and compose myself, but it came out as a kind of mad shout. So, I'd effectively dribbled on her and then shouted in her face. She asked if I wanted to come and stay with her for a bit in her spare room. Oh God. I said yes.

November 12th – Dr Molly Beaujolais

Just spent £379.45 on shoes and £79.36 on suspenders and hair ribbons. I feel like Kitty Bennet's sexually promiscuous cousin. I'm afraid to move in case it costs me more money. Or breathe. Is there a tax on this air? There's a pox on my throat, Vincent has given me his cold. He's coming over in a minute and I haven't told him about Johnny. I'm not sure I'm going to cope – my two great loves under one roof. He's moving in tomorrow.

It will come in handy for the brother/ sister lover scenes in *'Tis Pity She's a Whore.* Been reading through the play with Vincent, trying to work out the staging. He always insists on playing the monk for some reason. I think he just likes wearing my choker. I wouldn't mind if he took up a vow of chastity for a few days to be quite honest. He's been improvising some surreal scripts of his own during sex lately – last night he tried to spark up some kind of bizarre call and response which went along the lines of: 'what do we want?' (that's where I'm invited to reply with fun or some explicit suggestion – preferred response would be: a cup of tea and a nice sit down) followed by 'when do we want it?' (Answer: 'Now'). I'm not sure it is what 'we' want. He said 'that's disgusting' to himself, after he rounded things up the other night. It's like shagging the Queen on the set of *Fun House.* Well, if it was good enough for Pat Sharp, the chemistry between him and Melanie Grant (90s television royalty) was undeniable.

November 13th – Dr Jonathan Nylon

What fresh hell is this? I am lying awake in a room full of Ronald McDonald's shady Sicilian relatives. I can't sleep because a moon beam is being refracted through one of the glass clowns' shiny eyeballs directly into my distressed dilated pupil. I have entered Schoenberg's

Pierrot Lunaire and the orchestral accompaniment is playing out in my mind. The string part, in particular, I can hear very clearly within the tinnitus ringing, and feel acutely upon my shredded nerves.

November 14th – Dr Molly Beaujolais

D Day. Oh Dear Day. OD Day. Ordeal Day. Audition Day. The students (inmates) filed in, in varying contorted shapes and deranged states – ranging from excessive vulnerability to sociopathic enthusiasm. It was like a roll call of my ex-lovers.

I lit a cigarette after Dido's extended friar scene. It was positively postcoital. I know I shouldn't smoke in there, but I needed to get rid of the smell of Lynx Africa and failure.

'Bring in the next victim,' I called.

The Cat bounded in. Full of it (not the text – he couldn't remember a word of that). Full of shit. I had already mentally cast him as Vasques, he seems the candidate most likely to be capable of murder. His audition was 60 per cent improvised, 40 per cent heavy breathing – it was like an inexperienced call girl's first shift. I think he was imagining the object of his vengeance was the CEO of Wrigley's Extra, because he spent most of the time gazing maniacally at a piece of chewing gum on the ceiling. I offered him a polo on his way out for his troubles.

Robert Galloway was ten minutes late for his audition because he was braying loudly about the benefits of Brexit for capitalism. He was wearing his old Eton blazer. True to type and I cast him as such – the brother, secretly in love with his sister.

Florence is the best-looking girl in the class and was asked to try on Robert's blazer/hat ensemble after the audition, if the overpaid, underworked cap owner's cap fits. She will play Annabella (the sister).

A man who has not attended a single class turned up and gave an erratic, but amusing audition for Poggio. If he can reign in his voice to be contained within the 4-5 note range common to most human beings, he should do well in this comic role. His interpretation of the character as it stands is like a John Cage vocalise, complete with schizophrenic cadenzas – followed by his four minutes, thirty-three seconds of silence. There is a distinct lack of camaraderie within the group.

The others were not worthy of note. It was an effort to remember their names – before I wrote them on bits of paper and picked them out of a hat.

November 14th – Dr Jonathan Nylon

5.30 am – (Molly's spare room.) I'm awake. I feel as if they have all turned to face me in the night, although there's no way; it's one of those things where the eyes follow you round the room wherever the subject is stationed, these characters' eyes are all at odd angles from their faces. I feel like Bilbo in that bit where the dwarves are gathered around him discussing how best to eat him. Do clowns eat people? I don't know who I'd ask about that. I had an opportunity to ask Vincent in the hallway on the way to the bathroom but thought better of it. We talked about politics instead. I don't know why she thinks he's so clever. I asked him his views on Brexit, 'Deal or no deal?' and he said he can't stand the show and he doesn't believe in TV. What a moron and how can you not 'believe' in TV, I hate it when people say that – it's existed since 1927. What is his deal?

10 pm – I asked Molly about the clowns. At first, she said she's had enough of clowns for one day, but then she relented and explained their backstory to me – wherever they originated from, I wish they would go back from whence they came! She said they are Murano clowns from Venice, and she's inherited them from her Nan. Old people can be so cruel.

November 15th – Dr Molly Beaujolais

Thought I'd got through the week without talking about Nathaniel Bucket, but no week is complete for Alec without a detailed dissection of the man.

He approached me in the canteen, he'd heard a documentary on *Women's Hour* about Maria

Zambaco, who died in Paris in 1914 and was friendly with Rossetti and that lot. Apparently, she'd made some serious artworks, such as tabletop ice sculptures. He was curious to know if these were usually considered "serious artworks". He then wanted to know if all Nathaniel's pieces were serious and philosophical or did he write comedy ones as well.

'He liked a laugh,' I said.

'Oh?'

'He was a regular at Le Chat Noir.'

'So did he write anything about his times there?'

For God's sake Alec. Let the man have a drink in peace, without having to churn out some work and let me eat my chicken schnitzel salad.

'Yes,' I said.

'What was it called?'

'*Le Chat du Gare.*'

'He likes puns our man Bucket, doesn't he?'

'Yes, what's wrong with that? He was very in tune with the people.'

'The fin-de-siècle hoi polloi.'

I'm just ignoring him now, I think he just likes saying 'fin-de-siècle', probably the only French he knows – and I'm fairly sure I taught him that – by rote! I tried to turn away from him slightly, but he carried on staring at my back.

'It's about a cat,' I turned to him and said.

'Oh! I thought it would be about a fin-de-siècle racing pigeon.'

'There are other animals in his life.'

I made the mistake of mentioning once that Nathaniel owned racing pigeons back in Basingstoke and was very attached to them.

'He lived on the rails,' I said.

'Who, Nathaniel Bucket, fallen on hard times has he? Or is it the cat – has the cat fallen on hard times?'

I paused. I thought I'd leave it ambiguous for a moment. I wish Nathaniel Bucket would bloody fall on hard times, throw himself on the rails and take me with him! I thought he'd get bored and scuttle off to his office, but he just kept staring at me, and grinning like a bloody Cheshire cat himself, so I answered, 'the cat.'

'In between the rails, surely.'

I took a mouthful of schnitzel and bought myself some time.

'Yes, in the evening.'

'And in the day?'

'He lives on them,' said.

'Oh aye. What does he do on the rails during the day?'

'When there are no trains,' I said (he wasn't catching me out again),'he walks along them.' Two plays where there is no action in one half because of mortality or injury would be too farfetched.

'Just ... walks?'

'No, walks ... with purpose – like a tightrope walker.'

'You could argue that tightrope walkers walk quite tentatively,' he said.

And then I just pretended to have a coughing fit and walked out of the canteen, abandoning the remaining schnitzel. Walked out and down the hall as far away from him as I could – simultaneously with and without purpose.

12 am – I've just had a dream that Nathaniel Bucket and I were engaged in a duo trapeze act. He was walking towards me with desperate eyes, holding out a pen and parchment in front of him, while a pigeon pecked at the rope. Vincent is working late on his exhibition again; I can hear Johnny calling out in his sleep next door. I think he's singing Sondheim actually. He'll have to thrash it out alone, I cannot offer him a

lifeline today, my nerves are as frayed as Nath's rope. 'Not my circus. Not my monkeys,' as the Polish say.

November 16th – Dr Jonathan Nylon

I've had Bernadette Peters singing *Send in the Clowns* going round my head all day. Missed Remembrance Sunday last week so tried to have a moment's silence with the old fogies at the allotment. A moment's peace! It didn't last long, Terry had accidentally chopped one of Margot's carrots in half and she threatened to enact the same punishment on him. He mistook the purple variety for a gnarly clod of earth. 'This Dark Ages prison has no steel bars, chains, or locks. Instead, it is locked by misorientation and built of misinformation.' I hope I can apply Bucky Fuller's theory of ephemeralization to my sanity – I am having to do more and more with less and less each day.

Talking about being spread too thinly – brain cells being spread too thinly, I encountered Vincent in the kitchen this morning, we had an awkward moment negotiating who would use the toaster first. He won.

He is a very peculiar man. He toasts his butter. Not as in raises a toast, although I suspect he has a drink problem to boot. He doesn't butter his toast; he toasts the butter – he holds the knife with the butter on it and applies the toast to it. He is all kinds of wrong.

I also saw Molly, emerging from the bathroom in a towel. There are no words. Well, I couldn't think of any at the time.

November 17th – Dr Molly Beaujolais

Shoe count: forty-seven and a half (found a pair of vintage pony-print, backless heeled mules on eBay). Vincent asked me to walk across his chest in them when they arrived this morning. I trotted with great trepidation over his delicate rib cage, like the third (heftiest) billy goat trying not to fall through the wooden slats. Michael Jackson's 'Bad' had just come on Steve Wright's *Sunday Love Songs* (an unusual choice). He likes to keep his listeners on their toes, our Steve, he rarely spoils them with a sentimental selection. More often than not, he gives them what they need to hear, not what they want and I'm sure they're better off for it. Poor Margaret from Evesham who was calling to request a song to celebrate her son's engagement ("at long last") was given 'Cupid's Chokehold' by Gym Class Heroes. I found the syncopated rhythm of 'Bad' very off-putting for strutting down the catwalk of Vincent's torso – it made me stoop and stride in a stuttery fashion. Less nimble billy goat, more Bambi on stilts: a billy goat doing the trip trap of shame, perhaps, or a chastened Nijinsky, après l'après midi du drinking.

I could hear some strange tinkering going on next door – you could be forgiven for thinking a cheeky Morris dancer was attempting to join in the festivities, such was the cacophony going on. It was Johnny, pootling about in the spare room – when I stepped outside my door, I knocked over a cup of tea he had made for me and left on the floor outside. I caught him disappearing down the hall, clutching a Murano clown – he was holding it quite roughly, by the top of its multi-buttoned glass shard of a hat. I hope he didn't hurt himself. My heart still yearns for him, but

Cupid has me in a chokehold. Also, I've heard that Wendy used to be barrelling champion of the Devonshire region, whatever that means. I might put a request in to Steve – clear up some of the confusion surrounding my wants and needs. Not that I will be able to act on them, with my svelte, log-like torso, Wendy could fling me from Seaton to the Scilly Isles.

November 17th – Dr Jonathan Nylon

I've been trying to prepare a lecture on the celestial spheres for my medieval students, but I can't concentrate with the clowns in my physical and psychological orbit. I've given them names corresponding to the planets as depicted by Dante in his *Paradiso* chapter.

I need to direct my mental energy somewhere besides my present reality. Michael Jackson's 'Bad' is playing next door and the offbeat rhythms are doing nothing to conceal what I can only assume is rampant lovemaking or manslaughter (is it appropriate to make love to Michael Jackson, I'm not sure).

Here's what I've managed so far:

The Moon (The Inconstant) – 'Watch out Beetles about' – the one with the beady eyes, his refractive orbs exhibit the same optic tricks that Beatrice mentions when describing the moon's surface. His skin texture is also pockmarked, there is a hole the size of the Sea of Tranquillity on his right cheek. Molly said that a few of them were used as target practice by her Uncle Neil when he was a boy. He should've used stronger pellets.

Mercury (The Ambitious) – 'Alfie Feather Boa' – this waif-like fellow has an air of arrogance about him, he also does good out of a desire for fame like the Sun's closest neighbour. He wears a lilac feather boa, and his face is orange. Too much time loafing under the sun's hotbed of vice.

Let Ghibellines pursue their undertakings

beneath another sign, for those who sever

this sign and justice are bad followers.

His company is best avoided. His arrow-like eyebrows point the other clowns in the direction of avarice and vanity.

Venus (The Lovers) – there are no lovers, but there is a character wrapped around a pole who seems very attached to it. I call him 'Catchpole'.

The Sun (The Wise) – 'Buddha' – this bowl-shaped creature has a curious appendage sprouting from his head, similar to the one Buddha developed post enlightenment – the chatra (parasol) or 'horn jewel' I think they call it. Unfortunately, he has an idiotic and demonic expression on his face, so this is where the analogy falls down.

Mars (The Warriors of the Faith) – 'Ronald McKinney' – this one's eyebrows are at such an angry angle they cannot be contained on his face alone and stick out the top like antennae. His mouth is slightly open, poised for bemoaning, like Dante's ancestor Cacciaguida.

Jupiter (The Just Rulers) – 'Brioche Blessed' – a very rotund character with a long beard and kindly expression.

10 pm – I had to cut the exercise short as 'Ronald McKinney' fell from the cabinet – luckily, he survived the fall, eyebrows intact, I'm not sure I could recreate that expression. However, one of the buttons has come loose from his hat.

4 am – had just gotten off to sleep – it took me three hours to reaffix the miniature button. A vivid dream woke me up. Boris Johnson decreed that the playing and listening to of Michael Jackson tracks, hitherto widely enjoyed by lovers and singles alike, are now banned. Protests across London and the UK at large led to Gareth Malone forming a breakaway group, which managed to lobby for an act to be passed that allowed arrangements composed by himself of MJ's numbers to be permitted. They were not popular, and protests continued. The scene then cut to a heaving mass outside Westminster, I was caught at one end of the angry throng, Molly was stationed an arm's length away. I reached out to grab her hand and pull her to

safety, but a Marcel Marceau type character suddenly side stepped across her path, he performed some bewitching mime/vogueing movements and then she was gone. I heard a voice in my left ear, that of the student admirer. He whispered, 'who's bad?' I woke up immediately, arms flailing and smashed 'Ronald McKinney' sitting innocently on the bedside table to smithereens.

November 18th – Dr Molly Beaujolais

I thanked Johnny for the tea on my way out today, he looked very flustered – he was cradling something in a bundle of creased up newspaper. I said, 'I'd want you in my trench.' He blushed and looked me up and down nervously and replied, 'I don't think you'd fit.' I said, 'oh no, I meant metaphorically speaking, as in, if there was a war on ...' I could feel my face flushing. I shouldn't wear my coat inside; you don't feel the benefit. My cheeks burned against the cold, when I stepped outside.

6 pm – rehearsal was delayed with students complaining about their love lives – I'll be playing Paddy McGuinness at this rate. They've chosen a theme and it's *Take Me Out.* Other suggestions were 'Brexit, Things beginning with B' and 'Tarts and Vicars' – they have misunderstood, again. The Cat is concerned because he is unsure whether he is an otter or a bear. As long as he turns up to rehearsals as Vasques, I don't care if he's the fucking meerkat from the 'Go Compare' adverts.

Some kind of, albeit not normal, order will hopefully resume on Thursday.

November 18th – Dr Jonathan Nylon

I found myself next to my student admirer in the gents' urinals today, to my great horror and alarm. I'm not sure why I feel the need to specify I was in the *gents'* urinals, I'm fairly sure they don't have urinals in the ladies 'loos. I may start using their safe cubicles in future, I could do with the extra privacy and peace of mind (albeit provided by only a thin veil of **MDF**). I doubt earthly matter could deter him; I'm beginning to think he would rip through the veil to the tabernacle of the Holy of Holies if I was cowering on the other side of it. He didn't obey the 'at least one urinal separation' rule and as I left, he slipped a couple of walnuts into my pocket.

The lecture beforehand had been on the 'doctrine of signatures', outlined in Jakob Böhme's book *The Signature of All Things* and advocated by numerous other crazies of the Dark Ages. The main thrust of the argument is that certain plants bear a resemblance to certain body parts, animals or objects, and can be applied to those parts or ingested to stimulate the healing process.

The walnuts were wrapped in a tissue paper notelet, it read:

So delicate, they could crack in my hand

Autumn has come my love,

It will be you next

P.S If you don't go out with me, I will pickle my walnuts in brine. I hope they will keep 'til summer, when I will ask again, with the sun in my eyes and the shade upon your straight, yet supple back.

I think he has spent too long under the sun lamp, if the sun is in his eyes, it will also be upon my back – presuming we are facing each other. And my back is not straight or supple – I'm positively bent double these days with all the creeping about I've been doing at Molly's house. Also, the walnut is symbolic of the brain – his is clearly fried!

November 19th – Dr Molly Beaujolais

Had to rush to Boots this morning to get Vincent's Margate photos developed before class. He insisted on taking them with a disposable camera. He said the disposable camera is the instrument of the millennial Renaissance; he is not just taking photos, he is ushering in a new artistic age. I said they will take an age to come through, but he didn't see the funny side.

I nipped into the one in Farringdon. There is a curious and highly revered sales assistant working there, a soft-spoken Scottish character, he has his own fan page. He sounds a bit like Mrs Doubtfire and does a lot of unnecessary hand gestures when serving you – like a magician – the receipt is his main prop. How to collect points, card points – the main crux of his patter – the hand gestures and the patter are on a continuous loop; it has a hypnotic but jealousy-inducing effect (the script is the same for every customer). You'd never get anything done if you worked with him, like having the radio and the TV on at the same time. I usually try to avoid his till (my habitual preference being for speed over emotional exchanges). I feel bad about that, but I think it's a mutually beneficial arrangement: he has other customers who can meet his needs and I have other assistants who can meet mine.

'Are you from the 90s?' said the not-so-kindly female shop assistant next to him. At first, I thought she was referring to my head-to-toe Urban Outfitters ensemble, then I realised she was referencing the disposable camera.

'They're for my boyfriend,' I said.

'Oh yeh?' She said, raising an eyebrow, and we shared a little moment, a knowing naughty giggle. Mr Doubtfire handed them to me with a florid gesture resembling a magician brandishing a deck of cards – a trick deck. Luckily, I was out of the shop, and out of their view when I opened the packet – they were all of Vincent.

9 pm – we've decided to crack on with some Christmas repertoire at choir – there is some talk we may do a few traditional wassailing numbers at the staff Christmas party, which is to be held at a karaoke bar in Soho – so that won't be out of place at all. Cudjoe suggested Feliz Navidad, but Alec shuddered so hard at the suggestion his gilet fell off, so that has been vetoed. The carols McKinney has sourced seem to be

designed to create a humbug atmosphere of festive ill will, they are so obscure, and the tunes so bland, not a single soul on earth could pick them up. When he left, I picked them up, however, and put them straight in the recycling bin – they will probably be reproduced as a policeman's notebook, or something equally severe. They are punishing.

Talking of punishment, I tried to deter McKinney from inflicting the wassailing dirges on the people of Soho before he left, and he managed to steer the conversation back to his favourite subject.

'I haven't heard of these carols Alec, do you think they may be too obscure?'

'I haven't heard of Nathaniel Buckett – but I am pleased you've introduced him into my life.'

'Well, yes.'

'So how come he's never been discovered?' He persisted.

'Well he has, but only recently.'

'Where did they find him, in the Thames? That's where I'd put him if he made me sit through that chat du shite.'

'In between the pages of a book at Basingstoke library, actually,' I said.

'Oh aye? Which book then? One in the Children's section? How come it hasn't been found until now?'

'Well, they weren't't expecting to find him there.'

'Oh I don't know, I think that's the first place I'd look.'

If anybody needs to look for me, I'll be in the Thames. With any luck, fully immersed and then reborn as one of Nathaniel's Texan ancestors, before the days of transatlantic travel and universities.

November 20th – Dr Jonathan Nylon

I caught Vincent trying to 'develop' some photos in a vat of Waitrose own bleach poured into a painting tray this morning, under the heady glow of an ultramarine lava lamp. I walked straight in and turned the light on. He screamed, 'No!' I said, 'I don't understand' and he said it was part of the process. The mental rehabilitation process, I hope. A bird was screeching in the background, it sounded like cats being routinely murdered. Nature is thrown into disarray in his presence, he offsets the natural balance of things. He offsets my natural balance for sure, I haven't been able to use the toilet for days. He's always in there, conducting his two-hour morning levee. His cornucopia of creams takes up half the sink space as well, I can barely fit my slim toothbrush in between his IsoSensuals ('Butt Enhancing Cream') and Kiehl's Midnight Recovery.

I still haven't fully recovered from the midnight mayhem at my last abode. I have exchanged one mad artist for another. I've jumped from the frying pan, unenhanced butt first, and into the fire – with all the carcinogens hanging about in the air, I'm surprised we haven't all gone down in flames. Thought I'd got away from all that.

November 21st – Dr Molly Beaujolais

My students are going to need a lot of directing, I can see that now – shepherding. I might invest in a crook for Dido. He retreated behind the door before his scene with Annabella today. He said he was imagining he was in the confession box. I suggested he just imagine the set without visual aids for the time being, there is no need to use actual objects. Which he interpreted as an instruction to crouch down and start moving his hand horizontally in a stroking motion, then shift to a slightly more upright position with his hand lifted to his brow and peer up at the ceiling – he performed this sequence several times in quick succession. He looked like a World's Strongest Man contender during the stone globe event, tossing up whether to compete for the title or relieve himself in the toilet. 'What are you doing?' I asked.

'I thought there might be animals on the Isle of Fernando's, small mammals and birds?'

'No, no mammals and the birds are not visible in this scene,' I said. Florence got to her knees, crossed herself and began her confession. Meanwhile Dido was performing body rolls.

'What are you doing, Dido?'

'Could there be dolphins?'

'No, there are no animals, aquatic or terrestrial. Why do you need there to be animals?'

'Because I'm a friar,' was his answer. Long pause. 'You said to research our characters and create a back story – I'm Friar Francis of Assisi.'

'You're Paddy McGuinness. Do as I say today, not yesterday,' I said.

More ludicrous improvisation than you'd find at Tory hustings. I have given them far too much free reign and not enough information about the free psychiatric services provided at the university.

November 22nd – Dr Jonathan Nylon

Met with George for a drink at The Sylvan Post this evening. He was sent to cover the heartwarming tale of Faith yesterday, the brindle Staffy, who had almost lost hers – her faith that is in the yoke of human kindness and hope of finding a loving home to while away her remaining years. 'Not many left probably, she's been institutionalised for so long,' said George.

'Who? Demelza? Is that why she works freelance?' I jested.

'It was awful Johnny, she tried to interview the dog. 'Just to give the story some colour,' she said.'

'How did that go down?'

'Oh, like a lead balloon, Johnny. She said: 'she's very quiet, is she traumatised? Norfolk must be a very different environment for her, harsher. How is she adjusting? She started life dodging traffic on a beautiful Bath Roman Road, now she will find herself dodging shotgun bullets on a muddy Norfolk trail. Or Northern people,' she said to me, in a not-so-sotto-sotto voce. 'Write that down, George,' she added, 'but not the last bit.' Christ. The wife got a bit teary, and I had to comfort her. I made a pot of tea and was about to offer it round, when Demelza said, 'None of that Yorkshire crap for me, thanks.'

I told him about Wendy. I'm thinking I need to try and make a go of it with her – get over Molly.

'I think you should give that student a chance, Johnny. He sounds like he'd be cracking in bed – very attentive.'

Give him a chance to defend himself in court more like, that is more than he deserves. I showed George some of the illustrations and he said he is a very talented artist and enquired as to why I've kept them.

'I don't like to discourage my students in their intellectual and artistic endeavours.'

'Christ Johnny! Give them a good grade, don't put their sexually explicit artwork on your fridge.'

'I'm sentimental,' I said. I went to dispose of them in my empty pint glass, but

George hastily snatched them out my hands and slipped them into his pocket. I would never give him a good grade. I always give him 2:2s. I gave him a 2:1 once and he came up behind me when I was attempting to leave the lecture hall and sang '2 Become 1' by the Spice Girls into my left ear in a husky baritone. I would give him thirds, but I couldn't face him for another year.

11 pm – I popped into the corner shop to buy more butter on the way home, Vincent has cleaned us out. When I got home, I realised I had picked up a kilo of Maris Pipers and put them into my bag by mistake. It

must be subconscious sexual desire rearing its ovoid head. Called Wendy and arranged a date for Sunday.

November 23rd – Dr Molly Beaujolais

Tesco is getting very bourgeois; I overheard a woman requesting her groceries be put on her tab today. 'Just put it on my tab,' she said to the bemused checkout boy. The standards are hardly Liberty's Food Hall however – I spotted a batch of jam doughnuts on my rounds, with no sugar on and none in the tray! I got in the queue with my baked beans, bread and bag of sweet treats. A dishevelled looking man in a flannel robe was shouting at the till, he grabbed hold of my teddy coat, but then let it go and gestured graciously to the free till next to me – I thanked him and sneaked him a sugar free doughnut. The tab lady started kicking off about the length of the queue and then segued unexpectedly into Elon Musk's Cybertruck – she was concerned hurling sledgehammers and steel balls at car windows would incite acts of vandalism and also that he should be wearing a suit if he's going to go "on the telly". (I assume she means the news. If so, I'm not sure Elon prepared for that either.) The robed man, hitherto cheerfully whistling, began going off like a camping kettle. She was talking to the wrong audience. I saw she had a bag of the déclassé beignets – the checkout boy, who was rolling his eyes previously, shot the delicatessen girl a look – perhaps licking the sugar off the loose doughnuts is the new 'spitting on your onion rings'.

November 23rd – Dr Jonathan Nylon

Dropped in on the old folks at the allotment, I've been neglecting them a bit lately – opting out of the Sunday evening socials Leslie has introduced. It usually takes me the rest of the weekend to recover from Saturday nights spent with Wendy, in my defence. The emotional strain makes me too tired for strenuous physical work. When Margot saw me, she took my hand and bowed her head into it, like an obsequious royal subject. I felt guilty for not attending the committee meeting on Thursday, but then she told me that I have unnaturally soft hands, "for a geezer" – a double-edged sword, double edged spade! I've been off the Jojoba hand cream for over a month now, I don't know what she's talking about! My sense of remorse frittered away fairly quickly after that.

1am – had a nightmare about the clowns. I knew it was coming. It began with Vincent filling up a bath for me with Waitrose own brand bleach and forcing me to enter. Disposable photos of key moments from my life were displayed on the shower rail. A Matey bottle of bubble bath in the guise of the head honcho clown (the large, looming one with the out-of-kilter eyes) was perched menacingly on the side of the tub – the rest of the clownish contingent were dispersed in the water like children's bath toys. Vincent then picked up one in a lilac ruffle shirt with a particularly lopsided gait and grin and held it close to my face – like Buffy wielding a cross at a vampire. It had the effect of driving me deeper into the bleachy waters – I tried to grab a hold of the taps or the side, but my hands were too soft to take a hold. That would have been a very opportune moment to wake up, but no, my unconscious mind had other plans. I slipped down the plug hole somehow and ended up in the murky sewers of Maida Vale. Wendy was there, she had taken the form of Splinter and was instructing a group of waistcoated steward turtles in mortal combat. Donatello smiled warmly at me and handed me a stick to joust with. And then I woke up – just as it was getting good!

November 24th – Dr Molly Beaujolais

I had anticipated I would be spending the evening with Johnny watching back-to-back episodes of *Take Me Out,* in the hope of accumulating some directing ideas, but he's not home yet. Vincent is working late on the exhibition as usual.

I'vee been slaving away in the kitchen for hours on end as well, making a Polish apple cake (recommended to Johnny by a man called Iwo, recommended to him by his 112-year-old mother – why a still young and potentially virile man wants to spend his fleeting days of youth discussing cake recipes with the elderly I don't know. I can't say I'm not relieved. I would be more bruised than these bottom-of-the-shelf fruits if he were to take a lover proper). The process involved painstakingly peeling six obscenely large Bramley apples, grating dough "as if it were cheese" and finely grating the zest of a lemon. My nerves are shredded. The lemon experience was the worst, I had to borrow one of Johnny's from the back of the fridge and it was like exfoliating the skin of a jaundiced old man. I hope he won't mind. I did call him to check, but it went straight to voicemail.

I got as far as the latest episode of *Take Me Out*, turned it off. It's not the same on your own. Unless you're with city banker Stephen, then there's not an awful lot of difference.

Went for a walk and passed the record shop. The windows were slightly frosted over, it resembled a scene from *The Old Curiosity Shop* (a BBC adaptation). I put my hand to the glass, little Nell seeking her little friend. Oh Johnny. A hand appeared on the condensation-covered pane – the channel had abruptly changed, and Freddy Krueger was now in the frame. Two shellac-coated nails took hold of the sign and turned it to closed.

I went home and watched the rest of Paddy's canon. Sola, abbandonata. No Pachelbel's canon and sweet chiming bells for me any time soon.

12 am – I still haven't heard Johnny's key in the lock. I'm not sure the cake will keep. A wedding cake it is not.

November 24th – Dr Jonathan Nylon

I'm writing this from the Skate Lounge of Somerset House. Wendy is taking a brief comfort break – from the long period of discomfort we've been in previous. If I die tonight, I leave my record collection to my niece Tilly and my heart to Dr Molly Beaujolais. I am sat here with a poor, crying child, who Wendy used as a stopper moments ago. Rather than reach for the barrier, like a normal citizen, Wendy's sportswoman instincts kicked in and she performed a perfectly executed version of The Rock's People's Elbow finishing move on the unsuspecting child. I've given the child a pen and a page from my diary, I can see he's drawn a succession of sad faces and what looks like a cumulonimbus cloud at sunset – I'm assuming that's Wendy in her white mohair coat and red (prematurely festive) jumper get-up.

I tried to adopt a cautiously leisurely pace, like Empress Matilda venturing out onto the frozen Thames during her Oxford Castle escape expedition, but I was overruled. Wendy has been haring around the rink at a rate of knots from the moment she stepped out onto the ice. She is wearing my sheepskin gloves. She wrestled them from me in the first five minutes and insisted on holding my naked frozen hands for the duration – a kindness and a cruelty. She looks like she's wrestled the Polar Bear of Tower

Bridge and is sporting his fur as a trophy; he would have come off worse, no doubt. The coat is twice the size of her muscular physique, I'm amazed there is so little traction between her and the ice, considering the total mass it is transporting. I was keen to keep hold of the gloves for warmth, but also because I've become quite self-conscious about my 'soft hands' lately. I hope they'll return to their former state of suppleness. Currently, they are frozen rigid into a bear claw.

It's the first time in my life I know exactly how I feel about a woman. I do not love her. I am not in love with her. I am not in love with the idea of being in love with her. I do not desire her. I do not desire to desire her. Perhaps, perversely, this means she is the love of my life.

5 am – (Wendy's house) Went to bed with Wendy. Drank seven eggnogs whilst waiting for her with the crying child and his angry parents. When she returned, she managed to placate the parents and rescue me from the scene. She suddenly took on a look of a sexy Mrs Santa Claus. I'm afraid Christmas came early.

November 25th – Dr Molly Beaujolais

No Johnny making tea in the kitchen this morning. Vincent is getting on my tits today. He said, 'If your feet were on your face, I'd still fancy you' – sometimes I wonder if even he believes what he's saying. I'm sick of men lying to me all the time!

Also, my bank statement arrived in the post this morning. I can't keep buying stilettos like they're going out of fashion! It's time to face facts. Stilettos fell out of favour with the female public when they realised they could avoid walking home on broken glass at the end of a night out by not wearing them in the first place. And would Vince carry a weighty pair of thigh-high suede boots in his rucksack for an entire evening for me on the tube from Maida Vale to Hyde Park Corner and then go through the embarrassment of having the bag searched by the sweet Science Museum staff and the snooty staff of the Marriott Hotel (who turned to me and said, 'no smoking in the room' and turned to him and said 'no prostitutes')? No, he wouldn't. He wouldn't even carry my Tesco carrier bag of baked beans and oysters the other day, even though my hands were red raw. He said the bag was chafing against his narrow legs. Well, he is chafing against my narrowing patience!

The bag wouldn't have chafed if he had on a pair of trousers designed to fit a man of his stature – he's taken to wearing pastel pedal pushers and pulled-up white socks lately. Even he is not comfortable, he can pull off the look. He keeps stopping in the street and readjusting the socks, nervously looking at passers-by like a sprinter with the gun to his head.

Called Nan (via shaky video chat from Les Parfums de Rosine, Paris) to ask for some advice and whether she wants to see Snow White the pantomime at the London Palladium. She said never to trust a man who never removes his socks, especially in bed.

'They should've been burning their socks when we were burning our bras in 1972,' she said, lighting her pipe off a Jo Malone Fresh Fig. 'Maple leaf-loving, tug-boat driving, sock-wearing bastards.'

'Palladium, not Canadian,' I said.

'Where were they then?' she continued, undeterred. 'Sipping espressos in Sicily half the time.'

'He wasn't born then Nan.'

'The patriarchy always has an excuse,' she said.

As far as I know, she didn't stay long at the protests anyway. She turned up in a lion fur stole to sing 'I am woman, hear me roar,' and was met with disdain and red paint from the other women. (Which must have been an effort to attain in the crowd and at short notice!)

She said it was bequeathed to her by Swedish game hunter and notorious philanderer Bror von Blixen-Finecke, said to have picked up many a wild cat at the Muthaiga Club.

'The unspeakable in pursuit of the inedible,' I said.

'He didn't always shoot them, some died of natural causes.'

'Well I doubt that. Like what exactly?'

'Syphilis,' she said.

November 26th – Dr Jonathan Nylon

According to the FDA's Standards of Identity, 21CFR131.170(e)(4), the yellow food colouring used in eggnog must not be so yellow as to give the impression that more egg yolks are present than there actually are. Where are the laws protecting innocent citizens against the presence of more alcohol than is actually advertised on the bottle?

6 pm – had a call from an Ice Marshall at Somerset House saying they found my phone encased within a block of ice at the side of the rink. It must have fallen

out of my pocket as Wendy attempted the Dirty Dancing lift on Sunday. It is no longer working, thank God.

November 27th – Dr Molly Beaujolais

I came into rehearsal yesterday to find Alec sat solemnly at the piano playing 'Last Christmas' with his right index finger. It was a very stilted performance, difficult to listen to. When I walked in, he looked up like a startled rabbit, misty-eyed and twitchy-tailed. 'Hello,' I said. He carried on staring up at me, with his finger still resting on the F key – thank F he'd stopped playing it.

'Are you OK?' I offered.

'I'm feeling a little out of sorts.'

'Oh no,' I said, 'anything I can do?'

'Perhaps, a tale?'

'A tale?'

'One of Nathaniel Bucket's?' I'm sure I saw a maniacal glimmer flash across his iridescent irises, just for a split second. Perhaps he knows.

'OK, but this is the last one,' I said, like a parent negotiating with a petulant yet literature- hungry child, 'that I know of. It's called *A Tale of Two Skivvies.*'

'Oh aye, he's ripped off Dickens there,' he said, back to his old furbacchione ways – I began to regret my act of kindness.

'No, tale with an i,' I said.

'So, these skivvies, they have tails, do they?'

'A tail.'

'A tail between them?'

'A tail between their legs,' I clarified. 'A furry tail. '

'Oh aye,' he said.

'A tail that joins them,' I explained.

'Like an umbilical cord?'

'Yes.'

'From their arses?'

'Yes.'

'So, what happens in this play?'

'They just ... they find a way,' I said.

'A way to ...?'

'A way out.'

'Out of?'

'A lift.'

'Well, that's going to be a short play,' he said.

'Well, no, because they get caught up.'

'Oh aye? Does it break then, the lift?'

'No, well yes – for a moment. And there is some dialogue.'

'Oh, so he's mastered dialogue now, this must be after *The Sound of Parlance* then. How else do they get caught up? In emotion?'

'No, around a person.'

'Where's he then?'

'In the middle.'

'When did he get in the lift?'

'Nobody knows.'

'Just at some point,' he offered. 'Or maybe he's always there?' He's started adding his own embellishments now!

'They get caught up around him,' I said.

'What does the chappie do then?'

'He's quite polite about it, but there is a scuffle.'

'Not that polite then,' he said.

'Between the two tails,' I said.

'A wee brawl between the two tails.'

225

'Yes.'

'How do they stage that?'

'With puppets.'

'So, there's an extra man in there. '

'Yes, but he wears black and doesn't speak,' I said.

'Is he a stagehand chappie from *Parlance*?'

'Probably, actors often doubled up roles. One role becomes two.'

'I thought it was one tail between the two. One becomes two or two becomes one?' He queried.

'One becomes two – they get separated in the commotion, when they try to get past the man, it splits the tail in two, it's a very dramatic scene. The final scene,' I said. (God!)

'And they fight?' He prompted. He knows the play better than me.

'They're trying to reconnect, but yes, some critics say they're fighting – that is the surrealist element.'

'Oh aye, so these tail puppets – how do they work then, are they on strings?'

'No.'

'What are they on?' He persisted.

'His arms.'

'So, this chappie has his hand up two puppets and his shoulders up against the skivvies' arses? Is he double jointed?'

'It's a very small lift.'

'Doesn't his torso break the tail, the illusion of the conjoined tail?'

'No,' I said.

'Just ... No,' he said. 'OK, so it's very dramatic, I can sense that, aye. So ... Christ, does the third chappie help? Staunch the wound?'

'No.'

'Why?'

'Because he got out the lift.'

'He just walks out, with all that going on – in the middle of a medical emergency – he's to blame, getting in the way and starting on them. That is ... fucking, allagrugous.'

'No,' I said.

'What does he do then?'

'Slides out.'

'Oh, eey, there's a slide now – so these two skivvies are bleeding to death and he's pissing about on a slide ay?'

'No, he accidentally slides out.'

'Oh aye?'

'In the pool of blood.'

[Curtain].

'Quite a dark one for our man Bucket this time,' he said, softly.

'Yes,' I muttered, bowing my head.

Alec tenderly touched the piano keys and looked pensively at them. And then we had a moment's silence. For the severed tail I think, although it was hard to tell.

'Do the tails live on?' He asked.

'Yes, they live on,' I said.

It was a lie. It's all a lie.

November 28th – Dr Jonathan Nylon

Vincent was busy preparing for his exhibition this evening, so Molly and I had the flat to ourselves. It's been delayed, because he underestimated how long it takes to get disposable photos developed. Every time he found himself in the queue at Boots he kept walking out as well, which didn't help to expedite the process. Molly said he doesn't like rubbing shoulders with the Hoxton canaille.

We cooked a chicken cassoulet together and reminisced about the heady days spent at the record shop. I can't go in there anymore, because my student admirer has taken up a part-time position there. He is very sloppy at tempering the milk – I considered saying something the other day, it was almost stone cold by the time I found a table – but I didn't want to incite any racy banter about things steaming up etc. So, I turned on my heel and said nothing. I thought that might sever communication between us, but he is hell-bent on pressing my buttons. If he cannot have me, he will settle for humiliating me. Revenge is a dish best served cold and with lipstick still visible on the cup. I spent the whole morning walking about town with Rimmel rouge smeared across my chin.

We talked a bit of shop while the shallots caramelised. Molly's students have come up with a theme for their play, *'Tis Pity She's a Whore*. It's all about incest and priests apparently. The action is going to take place on the set of Paddy McGuinness' *Take*

Me Out and there will also be some scenes on the Isle of Fernando's. I've never met a friar from Bolton, but I'd estimate that they don't usually moonlight as comedians/game show hosts. I put this to Molly, and she snapped back, 'It's theatre,' as if that covers a multitude of sins. Perhaps Boris Johnson's PR manager should give that a go. I hear he used to dress as a chicken and improvise animalistic scenes for MPs, so he could always return to the boards himself, if the board pushed back. The father, Florio, runs the bar on the island – all the other characters permanently reside on the ITV set. She said she would like to do more – but didn't stipulate with what, I doubt she was referencing the play – she confessed most characters have been cast arbitrarily and she got Dr Branston to stand in for the second round of auditions, the man who thought *Starlight Express* was a new supermarket chain.

I'm not sure it quite works. Surely Florio could have procured his daughter a ticket to the Isle of Fernando's, without her having to be pimped out to all these randy wannabe holidaymakers. Seeing as he's the sole occupant on the island, he must have made a small fortune in the tourism trade.

These are the sorts of questions I would ask as a paying theatregoer. Molly said people who watch theatre don't ask questions, they let the actors on stage pose them and try to answer them later at the bar. So, I have narrowed it down to one question that I'm sure will also be running through the actors' heads – how long is the interval?

November 29th – Dr Molly Beaujolais

I couldn't get Robert and Florence to stop kissing during Poggio's scene today. I had to clap at them, like a frustrated park ranger trying to disperse copulating pigeons from his patch. Dido joined in, which changed the tone of the gesture and suddenly the whole class was egging them on with rapturous applause.

Spoke to Nan this morning before class, she's now in Vienna. She's been camping out at the apartment of Monika Salzer, founder of 'Grannies

Against the Right', after bonding in a biergarten on the Wien. She wants to come home to vote. Well, to "get those Tory bastards out" as she put it. She also wants to meet Vincent post-haste. He needs "sussing out", she says. She said she knew his grandfather, she met him in Venezia back in 1949 and he still owes her a fiver. She doesn't, she knew Charles de Beistegui, the art collector and interior decorator, and he contacted the family regularly since their meeting, asking that she call off 'the boys' and for a legitimate number to wire the money to. He was told the debt has been paid, but he wouldn't have it – Nan says it is the artists' twine that binds them. When he died in 1970, she arrived in Biarritz in a backless white gown and placed a five-pound note torn in two on the coffin. One half blew into the sea and the other landed in a lady's fascinator, and she pocketed it. My grandfather ran waist-deep into the ocean to retrieve the one half and asked the lady to buy him a drink at the wake to cover the cost of the other.

I sincerely doubt that he was buried on a beach. My grandfather maybe, I never knew him, but apparently, he spent most of his married life with his head buried in the sand.

December 1st – Dr Jonathan Nylon

Had a good laugh about the clowns with Molly today. Apparently, there is one named Heathcliff who is supposed to be cursed. They found him in the garden, reclining in a swallow's nest once, and no one knows

how he got there. She said if we got married, all this (gesturing to the grotesque glassy throng) would be mine. They would be going straight on eBay – they would probably have to be thrown to the bottom of a river and secured down with chains and locks, like the game Jumanji. She threw her head back and laughed maniacally at that. She laughs in the face of danger. A lock of her auburn hair grazed my bare forearm, I flushed like McDonald's boss Steve Easterbrook after being called out on his scandalous employee affair. You could've fried an artificially preserved burger on my face – if they weren't banned in the house by Vincent.

December 2nd – Dr Molly Beaujolais

NOTES – Act IV, Scene III – the putting out of Putana's eyes.

The lights are up, Vasques descends in the lift, he is dressed in overalls (he is employed as a racing car mechanic in ordinary life). 'Car Wash', the Christina Aguilera version plays out on the studio speakers.

In this scene the backstage dramas are revealed, Annabella's pregnancy and the rest.

I can remember very little from this play, despite being in it. I thought there was more romance, but it seems to be mostly violence and religious lectures. I think I've remembered it incorrectly because when I performed Annabella in Year 12 at St Thomas the Apostle School, Southwark, I was having a love affair with Tommy Howard, who played Bergetto on alternate nights and spent most of my time backstage, with him, operating the curtain pulley beneath his beautiful hands and only skulking out for my few scenes, if that.

I think the Banditti can be played by the audience. I expect they'll be feeling suitably positioned and motivated to maim an actor by this point in the proceedings. I'll give them a pre-show briefing. There is a disconnect between the words and the action at the moment, but I'm sure it'll all come out in the wash. Not the fake blood, however, I trialled it yesterday – that sugary shite has stained all my best tea towels! Although it must look convincing, I heard Johnny shriek when he tried to use one to take out his chicken Kiev from the oven last night.

The eyes can be put out during his (Vasques') compulsory 'party trick' moment – an accident with a flag display. Putana (a female contestant) will be dressed in a leopard print trouser suit, that barely covers her cougar body.

I'm thinking a video screen can play in the background at Vasques' line, 'for now comes your turn to know'. Then one of his mates can wax lyrical about him (as they do in the show – just a line or two of improv) and reveal at the end that the fun, but possibly off-putting fact about him is that he is a murderer.

Then black out.

I'm going to be needing a lot of those.

December 3rd – Dr Jonathan Nylon

Walked in on Molly in the shower. Not on purpose. Perhaps Freud would argue with that. She is perfection. I have struggled to concentrate all day. I don't think anyone noticed. I replaced any references to the ship Eidsvold in the lecture today with the words *my left testicle* and no one batted an eyelid. Not a single soul disputed that my left testicle was the first line of defence in the prelude to the battles of Narvik and was positioned 700 metres from Wilhelm Heidkamp during the German invasion.

It has been a full day of voyeurism, back-to-back unintentionally voyeuristic meetings with Molly. I disappeared into the basement in search of the most obscurely located lavatories at lunchtime and came across her conducting a lesson in one of the damp-ridden rehearsal rooms. It was like a scene from a Fellini film. She was sat on a chair smoking a cigarette, all I could make out was her hand holding it like she was holding a dart. A student shot across the safety-laminated door pane, his face was caked in white makeup, he looked like someone had drawn sad eyes on a mottled meringue. He turned his head so suddenly to look at me, it made me gasp audibly. Molly turned to me at the sound, and I scuttled away. I could barely taste my tortellini, dining in the canteen afterwards – for various reasons, but largely because I am sick with love for her. 'Life is a combination of pasta and magic,' as Frederico says. Or papier-mâché and menace in the students' case.

5 pm – Wendy called my office phone to check all is going ahead with our date on Monday. From being so prominently in the spotlight earlier in the day, suddenly my left testicle is nowhere to be seen.

December 4th – Dr Molly Beaujolais

Johnny walked in on me in the shower yesterday.
Vincent came in through the front door two seconds
after it happened. He has been away too long, I think.
Too long, but not long enough. I was bending down to
pick up the soap when Johnny walked in, I had my
bum against the glass – I don't want him to think I have
a flat arse. Two seconds more and I would've appeared
like the woman in the Herbal Essences' advert, my
hands running through my hair under a cascading
waterfall, bottom normally presented. As it stands, I
came across like a two-for-one promotion for
TRESemmé – two gluteus maximi for the price of one.

Vincent is taking me for a private pre-private
view showing of his exhibition later. I won't inform him
of my recent display of exhibitionism. He has quite a
jealous streak. A man who was marking our scores at a
pub quiz the other day leaned over me from his table
to change a mis-recorded bonus point and Vincent
broke his pencil in half. It was one of those tiny ones
you get in the scrabble box that you can barely hold, so
it was no small gesture.

12 am – I think I have just experienced the most romantic evening of my life to date. We wandered the exhibition's marble halls hand in hand, like the ghosts of Romeo and Juliet carousing in the mausoleum. Vincent had lit candles around some of the least flammable exhibits – a clay bust for example. We sat down beneath it and kissed. It is an odd sculpture – it looks as if the wheel has tried to throw it off a few times, the neck is leant back at a jaunty angle. With the candles, we must have resembled worshipers at the shrine of The Head from *Art Attack*. I'm not sure if this was the desired artistic effect. Vincent's potter's wheel is more temperamental than the waltzer at Blackheath funfair (in operation circa. 1999, built in 1962). In fairness, we were thrown off more times by the mechanic than the machinery, for not paying the fare – if we had, perhaps Billy, the owner, would have been able to afford the maintenance. The hamster wheel of poverty had ensnared us all. When we came to leave, Vincent said he loves me and that I am the woman for him. I hope he is still saying the same

things when he meets Nan on Saturday. She has just landed at Heathrow.

December 5th – Dr Jonathan Nylon

The Danny Dyer student approached me in the canteen and tried to engage me in conversation. I didn't hear a word she said. I was looking over her shoulder at Molly in the canteen queue.

Oh God, Molly. Molly's breasts. Molly's arse. Molly's breasts under the irritating trickle of water produced by her Homebase sale showerhead. Molly's bum pressed against the frustratingly small cubicle. Molly's tits covered by her tray as she contemplates the revolting rotisserie; Molly's bottom as she retreats from the salmonella-and-saline-solutioned salad bar. Molly's boobs ordering, Molly ordering an omelette over her boobs at the hot food section. Molly's arse stationed on the food tray rail while she waits in the impossibly long queue. Molly's nethers avoiding eye contact with one of my vertically challenged students who's dropped his chips. Molly's bosom brushing against his unfashionably gelled fringe as he stands up. Molly's womanly assets making their way towards me and into the view of another man, Dr Branston. Molly's fetching physique eclipsed by the mass that is pickled Branston. The front facing aspect of Molly's beautiful body between me and a cup of tea this evening, while we dissect the hilarity of the many hilarious scenes that have unfolded throughout the course of the day – in a state of pure joy and lust. Molly's arse again as she vacates the present scene, inevitably sullied by sexual frustration and disappointment.

December 6th – Dr Jonathan Nylon

I think I need to coax my brain into loving Wendy – rewire it. It is currently firing on all cylinders for Molly alone and my feelings for her are incompatible with daily life. I turned to Google for some assistance, and it suggests I may have 'obsessive love syndrome'. Here are some of the questions and my answers.

Q: 'Do your obsessive thoughts interfere with daily functioning?' A: Yes, they interfere with daily functioning, I now blank out everything my students say.

Q: 'Is your behaviour more erratic than usual?' A: Yes, I recently picked up a copy of Mills and Boon – *Tamed by the She-Wolf* from the university library and skipped straight to the last page.

Q: 'Once you begin a task are you always determined to finish it?' A: Yes and no – I have now completed the entire Anna Sewell oeuvre, but I cannot get to the end of this test.

It then asked for my bank details to receive the results, I could feel my obsessive penny-pinching syndrome flaring up at that point, so I switched it off and lost all my hard work.

I do like Wendy's accent. It's quite endearing as Southern accents go. I sometimes think us Southern English people, with our tawdry tones, have to work harder to win others' affections. When I was promoted to retail assistant at the meat factory, I once overheard a customer say to my colleague, 'You Southerners are all the same with your fuck-off attitude,'– the colleague

243

was from Belfast. I occasionally put on a Yorkshire accent in my darker moments actually, it puts me in a better mood for some reason.

December 7th – Dr Molly Beaujolais

Annabella and Giovanni are in love. Or is it Florence and Robert? They have no concept of the subtle art of building sexual tension. I have had to position Robert (Giovanni) under the stage for their opening scene, just to separate them. His character is a studio technician – I'm going to have him fiddling about with some cables at all times, to keep his hands off Annabella (Florence).

December 7th – Dr Jonathan Nylon

I am at Vincent's exhibition, thought I'd check it out solo. Just taking a break in the gallery cafe. Pacing the marble aisles in a state of high alert and stress, I felt more like a footman on a reconnaissance mission than a pleasure-seeking day tripper. Can you be your own muse? It is very Vincent-centric. It is nice to know that if I ever find myself wondering what Vincent de Boussay looks like from a 153.2-degree angle at any given moment, I can just dip into the visual catalogue I now have stored in my mind. There was no need to buy a postcard, I have the real thing at home.

I would like to see his head from a 360-degree angle however, turned all the way round in one swift movement and extracted from his shoulders preferably. I would pay £3.90 to see that immortalised in miniature print.

8 pm – I saw a character who looked very much like the Artist in Dissidence having a tête-à-tête and – I hope I'm mistaken but – a bouche bouche as well with some bird, just before I left. I don't know what to do. Molly seems so in love.

December 8th – Dr Molly Beaujolais

8 pm – Vincent has gone to bed early with Ozzy and Banger – Osama the Border Terrorist and Banger the Sausage Dog. Mr Fordy Man conked out at six and is still asleep on Mum's lap. It has been a harrowing day, for Vincent; he keeps telling me. I handed him a beautifully bronzed cup of char. He looked very peaky – we discovered that Nan had laced his eggnog with out-of-date Absinthe. I think it may have been intended as a kindly gesture. 'It's too dark,' he said. 'Everything is tarnished in this house, including the souls of its inhabitants. Tarnished and covered in carpet, carpet curtains, carpet on top of bits of carpet, even the lampshades are carpeted.' That is actually a William Morris original, but I sensed that it was not the right moment to speak up. Nan has christened him with the sobriquet 'Der Vampyr'. 'Pass the salt, der Vampyr,' she said at dinner.

'Don't keep calling him that, Mum,' I chipped in, 'you know he doesn't understand German.'

I stroked his temple and kissed his shell-like ear – he didn't move from the recovery position. I hope the mutts don't bite in the night; they can get a bit funny when they sense fear. I tried to get in next to him, but he turned away and drove his earphones deeper into his ears. They're very low quality, I could hear the monotonous rhythms of Einaudi pumping out.

You'd have thought he'd have had enough of him. There was a bit of an incident earlier. He sat down to play his Einaudi party piece at the spinet and Nan piped up with a request. We thought she was out, but she was sat there in the dark – it wasn't until Vincent switched on the lamp in the far corner that she became illuminated, like the *Woman in Black*.

'Play *Die Meistersinger*,' she gurgled from her velvet ochre armchair, spinning out every vowel and spitting the consonants.

'I can do that, Nan,' I said.

'No, it's fine,' Vincent retaliated in a quivering adolescent whimper. 'If you hum it, I can play it,' he persevered optimistically.

247

Nan then began humming in a peculiar fashion. It's difficult to interpret the precise meaning of her hums, this one is also the noise she makes when she wants another whisky.

'Let me do it, Vincent,' I said.

'Molly, it's fine,' he said, cracking slightly, 'I can do it!'

He couldn't do it.

Nan likes to imagine she's back in Bayreuth, listening to her many lovers in the chapel choir. I have to spread the chords to bring out all the parts and cross my right hand over to emphasise Oskar in the third desk tubas. He was, to coin the moniker to Rachmaninov's Prelude in C sharp minor, 'a dead man walking'.

December 9th – Dr Jonathan Nylon

Took Wendy to the British Museum – it is 'Old Person Monday' today (half-price tickets), there were floods of them – clogging up the galleries and the lavatories.

Wendy behaved like a rampant toddler and then criticised my outfit like a domineering parent – she had the cheek to say my paisley date shirt would look better with a tie, despite wearing a Christmas jumper with an actual 3D teddy bear on the front.

When we first arrived in the Great Court, Wendy formed a conga line of two with an eccentric gentleman who apparently circles the foyer all day as part of his morning routine (an indiscreet gallery assistant informed us). Wendy thought he (the eccentric gent) was the guide. The man shot her several withering looks and quickened his pace, but she was not put off. She pursued him all the way into the men's toilets, where she was eventually deterred by a member of staff – he addressed her formally as 'Madam', but there was too much questioning intonation in the salutation for it to be deemed polite.

We spent a few pleasant moments basking in the delicate sculptural wonders of the Hellenic age in the Parthenon Gallery, after I managed to steer her away from the more weapons-heavy galleries. Wendy took an unhealthy interest in the nether regions of the marble men and beasts. 'Even the horses have bollocks,' she said.

'Yes, horses in Ancient Greece had bollocks,' I replied. I was hoping to have the opportunity to explain something more intellectually advanced that might've showcased my extensive history knowledge, but it was not meant to be.

When we sat down to lunch, Wendy explained that the artefacts had inspired a joke for her comedy set. It all made sense now. Unbeknownst to me, throughout the course of the day she had been slipping into her stand-up persona in order to try out material. I hadn't twigged. I'd been so distracted all afternoon, thinking about Vincent and the mystery woman (I still haven't decided whether to mention it to Molly) that I hadn't noticed much of what she had been saying really. What I had noticed was that she had chosen to deliver a selection of sentences with a crazed, more intense expression, which caused me to feel a sense of inexplicable unease, but I could not say why. The unnerving habit first revealed itself at the security check in. 'Are you pleased to see me?' she purred. 'You've got something in your pocket?'

'No, no I've got nothing in my pockets,' I said. The security guard gave me a suspicious look. It took us an extra twenty minutes to get through the line after that.

The joke that had been hatched (I hope) when looking at the Parthenon frieze and went along the lines of, two horses walk into a bar ... I tried to adopt a neutral expression, one that is both supportive of Wendy as a person but damning of her as a comedienne – the sort that might cross the face of a police detective whilst interviewing a petty criminal.

'Long face,' I offered. Long pause.

'That's all I have so far,' she said. 'Do you think they'll like it?'

I'm not an expert in comedy, but it's my understanding that a joke can't just done piecemeal – it has to be conceived in its entirety.

'I think they'll be confused,' I said. 'But maybe they'll enjoy that. I don't understand people these days.'

'Because of the joke?'

Which joke? She needed to be clearer, she hadn't thus far supplied me with any jokes to refer to.

'The joke where there is one horse.'

'I think it needs more.'

'More horses?'

'More comedic material.'

I saw her cross out two horses and write three. She is a terrible student.

2 am – Woken up in a cold sweat. I can't be with Wendy, but I'll never be with Molly. I've come to the conclusion that I'm not her type – I'm not vegan or

artistic or evil enough. In truth I am just a boy from Bristol, who can't go more than four days without a roast dinner. That reminds me, must pick up a turkey from Morrisons for Christmas lunch with old folks next Sunday – that and the malnourished pigeon that's just flown into my window. Those turkeys are certainly not value for money – they might be the 'best' you can manage Mr Morrison, but they're not going to feed a ravenous throng of perennially persecuting pensioners.

December 10th – Dr Molly Beaujolais

Johnny is dating some absurdist comedienne! And I think Vincent has run away to Mexico – to live as a catfish. Joleen texted me about a man she's dating who looks like the gay one from *Made in Chelsea*. She sent me a picture. 'That is the gay one from *Made in Chelsea,*' I said. He'd sent her a dick pic. She sent it to me and it's Vincent. Then Joleen had it out with him, on the phone, not the street. I've had one lone text, ending it all and now he's gone on radio silence. Oh God. My heart is as hard as a stick of rock, the Basaltic

Prisms of Santa María Regla. At least I still have my obscure geography knowledge, which will come in handy if I ever decide to look for a romantic replacement – among the cast of *University Challenge.*

Oh God, he's coming back from the loo. Johnny that is. Think Vincent's fallen down a Xoxocotla long drop. I hope so! I hope an upright shard from a broken Mexican tile breaks his fall!!!

December 10th – Dr Jonathan Nylon

I told Molly about Wendy, I left out the bit about her being Mr McKinney's cousin. I think I wanted to make her jealous, but I made her cry. I told her that she's a comedienne and that she thinks I look like Michael Brandon from the Dominion Theatre cast of *White Christmas.* That's when she started crying. I said it is just a fleeting resemblance, and he's not the best-looking member of the cast by a long shot. And then she said Vincent's a bastard catfish, but I don't know what that means. Then she said the strange thing is she doesn't care that much, or as much as she would've thought. Although she was crying so much, I could barely make out what she was saying.

Then I said, I don't know what a catfish is, but it doesn't sound like a good thing and you're probably better off without one. I don't know what I was saying really. I love her. That's what I wanted to say. I made her a cup of tea and a strong cocktail of miscellaneous spirits, then poured myself a whisky into a tankard from St Ives. We talked until 2 am and then she took me into her room.

The bed posts were adorned with various silk scarves, ribbons and ropes; high heels were strewn about the floor and half-hanging off the bookshelves. A pair of suspenders lay tangled in a SCART lead. It was like Gok Wan had had a mental breakdown. She led me to the bed, put her hand on my chest and said, 'I'm sorry Johnny, but it's you.'

It cut through the air, which was quite an achievement, because it was dense with smoke and perfume. I suddenly felt like the little boy in that story, the one who gets so angry he disappears off somewhere altogether different – floating in his bed, space all around him. Everything I was angry about, all these years, just went away for a moment – like I knew how to get home.

Of course, I didn't. I had no idea how to get 'home' – to my room or how to get anywhere else – the whisky had gone straight to my head. And I have no idea how to love her, but I don't think it matters. And then she threw up all over my paisley 'date shirt'. 'It's better this way,' she slurred and passed out on the bed.

December 11th – Dr Molly Beaujolais

I think I died in the night. My mouth is a mausoleum.

Johnny and I haven't discussed the adventures from last night yet. When I awoke, he was gone and I was swaddled in a crocheted blanket, displaying a view of Palace Square, St Petersburg– my left toe was poking through a hole and delicately cupped by Pushkin's outstretched palm. Safe in the hands of poets past and present, Johnny had left me a note. It said:

You passed out

The stars were out, so it was time to crack the Tsars out

And like a Tsar and Soviet law, I hope you were also not bound too tightly (by the blanket I mean . . . although I noticed there were plenty of other binding materials knocking about! Which I didn't go anywhere near! Of course)

And that you slept well

In the loving embrace of Mother Russia

Popping out for more tea bags

I love him. I love him. I love him. I love him. (In Russian)

7 pm – Popped out to buy Johnny his Christmas and birthday present. He told me last night he was born on Christmas Day and always receives a combined

Christmas and birthday present. We are spending the evening together as well; hope he can handle it – he's used to receiving all his fun at once.

December 11th – Dr Jonathan Nylon

Woke up with a banging headache – it took all my strength not to insert one of the stray cocktail sticks strewn across the kitchen top into my tympanic cavity and end it all.

I've had to take my paisley shirt into town to get it dry-cleaned. The corrosive combination of red wine and stomach acid may have permanently stained the delicate fabric. Molly claims to be a lover of fashion, but she has displayed nothing but contempt for my shirt by throwing up all over it.

I'm at the dry cleaners now, but I'm having to wait – perched at the end of a mustard leatherette seat that looks as if it has never felt the warm caress of a hot wash in its existence. Oh, for goodness' sake, a middle-aged-to-aged French gentleman in a lilac floral blouse and a Le Coq Sportif baseball cap has just muscled in front of me. The lady on the till looked between us and enquired whether we are paying together. I don't give two hoots about Mr Phillipe's pension reforms; he's not getting a penny out of me – he seems to be wearing the Prada Pope's red loafers, for Christ's sake! The smile he gave me was not suggestive of a soul pure in mind and body, however.

Molly is at home in my bed, good Christ. What am I doing fraternising with this frilled, fraternal creature! Oh, he's finished, a decision has been made – he's going to go for a 'wash and fold' – fire up the white smoke!

12 pm – shite, forgot the tea. We finished up the booze instead. Because we're young and in love and it was a bottle of Prosecco. I love her. I love her. I love her! (In an Italian accent.)

December 12th – Dr Molly Beaujolais

Watched the *Muppet Christmas Carol* with Johnny. It was wonderfully cosy.

As the credits began to roll, he turned to me and kissed me. Then he said, 'I wouldn't leave you at the mercy of three ghosts.' He left me talking to three decrepit old biddies from The Forest Hill Foragers Society earlier, which was pretty close. If it was a date, it was the strangest one I've ever experienced. I spent two long hours foraging for signs of life in the undergrowth and there was none to be found there either. Is he saying he sees me as a Scrooge-like figure, I'm presuming he's cast himself as Dickens then (the author of my destiny). I happily consent.

Perhaps he's right – Dr Branston came round the campus dressed as Father Christmas the other day, shaking a bucket and singing 'Good King Wenceslas' at close range. The cause was the university. I contributed nothing, I'm ashamed to say, but felt compelled to take a few pounds out to go towards the cleaning bill for my pale pink silk shirt, it was doused in a very unfestive sprinkling of saliva and canteen crudité afterwards.

December 12th – Dr Jonathan Nylon

I kissed Molly.

We were watching the *Muppet Christmas Carol*. When we came to the bit where Kermit is escorting Tiny Tim home on his shoulders (before he comes a cropper on the ice) for some reason it launched Molly into a tirade about her disdain for weak and ineffectual men. It was an inspiring and motivational speech. Once the ghosts had departed, I knew it was the moment to exorcise my demons and make a move. I leaned over and brushed her hair from her face, my other hand got lost down the side of the sofa in my clumsy manoeuvring. There were a few crumbs from a chocolate hobnob cemented onto my index finger once the hand was dislodged, but she didn't seem to mind. She cupped the offending digit with her faultless fingers, then let me hold her face with both hands and kiss her again.

It was the first time I have wished the credits to a film were longer. It was a very tender moment. Tiny

Tim would have clasped his tiny frostbitten hands together in delight, had he seen it.

Afterwards we made our way to Essendine Primary School, hand in hand – to vote. The queue was longer than the one I'd imagine will already be forming at the Strangers' Bar, Westminster. We didn't notice the inconvenience, we kissed for the duration of the wait. An elderly man in a cravat had to poke us with a stick at one point. We dropped our folded papers into the ballot box – a penny in the wishing well for our rosy-hued future.

December 13th – Dr Molly Beaujolais

We rehearsed Annabella and Giovanni's fight scene today. I demonstrated some choreography ideas but was asked to stand down by the students and observe from the sidelines. I think I am experiencing some symptoms of sexual frustration that are manifesting as aggression – Johnny and I are yet to make love. Last night was the perfect moment, but he is holding back his moves. Dido, however, has a full routine ready to go that he is prepared to exhibit on every occasion – lifted from *Rush Hour 2*. This is not the first time he has recommended the moves of the masterful Jackie Chan, though always from the second submission to his *Rush Hour* canon. We have been going round and round with triple roundhouses. I wish he would put as much effort into observing the words/stage directions in his script as he does into observing Jackie Chan. Any variation would be welcome. I would settle for some moves from *Rush Hour 1* even, if I'm not going to be permitted to see the movement of the back of Dido's head exiting the stage on time.

Last week, under his directorial hand, Jackie was insinuated into the lovers' bedroom scene. Dido would not have it that the Jeet Kune Do block (or 'the way of the intercepting fist' as it translates) was out of place in a romantic setting. I believe I have personally experienced scenes from a *Drunken Master II* in many a bedroom scenario, but JKD I could not incorporate it tastefully. Perhaps I need to get Johnny down to the Red Dragon Casino. That's where all the action seems to take place.

December 13th – Dr Jonathan Nylon

The Conservatives are victorious – having conquered Labour's seats in the 'traditional heartlands' of the North and Midlands. I am nonplussed. My heartland has long been conquered and the only seat I care about today is the one I'll be taking next to Molly at the staff pub karaoke party later. Cannot wait for the moment when I walk in with Dr Molly Beaujolais on my arm. For the first time in my life, I won't need to enter a room casting my eyes about for the love of my life or the emergency exits.

December 14th – Dr Molly Beaujolais

Just had a call from McKinney saying steps may need to be taken to avoid the termination of my contract. Around 38 in total, he tells me – he has drawn up a list, as have the students (of complaints – the traitors! A petition they're calling it and it's signed by 25 of them). 38 steps, fuck me, that's a lot – one short of an adventure story though, unfortunately. Perhaps an adequate amount for *Journey to the Centre of the Earth*, I'm picturing McKinney and I taking 38 strides around the rim of Kilimanjaro followed by a nosedive into the centre of it. My career is set to bite the rust-coloured dust and it seems I'm to drag my musical accomplice down with me! He says it's better I see it in person – what will I be encountering – a scroll nailed to my office door like Martin Luther's 95 theses? Anyhow, the meeting is this afternoon.

7 pm – I take it all back, not McKinney and I's one way ticket to Tanzania – we'll be needing that yet. Well, I will, he could probably do with staying put for a while and saving some pennies. He confessed to me that he went on a trip to Basingstoke, via Basildon (that man needs to get his eyesight tested – I hear from Johnny this isn't his first rodeo in wrong directions!) and that the staff at the Milestones Museum of Living History of Basingstoke have never heard of Nathaniel

Bucket, and they should know. I said to him, 'Alec, darling, you should know, I no longer care. Save your steps, sweet man, buy a Fitbit with the money saved from my wages.' And then I tried to swoop off dramatically, but Alec had just rolled out the scroll and my exit path was curtailed. We still had to stagger through the small print, despite my heroic gesture to bow out gracefully. It turns out the petition was a joint effort, not between my students and their one mutually accessed brain cell, but by the class next door and the borough council! I knew it wouldn't be my own precious lambs, I've been nothing but a wonderful counsellor to them from day dot. The main complaint raised against me is one of 'excessive noise and disruption to the peace'. I was a fool to take this job – and veto the mime module.

I need to get away from it all. From them all. Johnny and his entourage of elderly people and acerbic, ailing academics.

10 pm – Called Luce. She's invited me to spend Christmas with her in New York. Perhaps there is another divine counsellor on this worldly ward.

1 am – Johnny is nowhere to be seen. But I've heard reports from Cudjoe that he is still alive and well. Probably out fighting, it is a Saturday night. Apparently, he did a rendition of Elton's classic last night, after I'd left the pub. He said the machine was glitching towards the end of the night, but the sped-up tempo didn't deter Johnny. In fact, he delivered the song with such aggressive impact that once the track had finished, he'd dropped the mic, but couldn't stop the leg-jigging/stomping motion he'd adopted throughout the whole performance. It morphed into a two-step, and he proceeded to steadily, but hurriedly march out the side emergency exit – still in time to the frenzied beat. Sandra said she saw him moving in the direction of campus, muttering Saturday repeatedly, with no signs of slowing or stopping. She couldn't tell me what happened next.

December 14th – Dr Jonathan Nylon

Woke up this morning on the campus lawn, dishevelled and streaked with white powder – like a subordinate in the court of Queen Anne, post orange pummelling. I have no idea what happened, all I know is that the evening was an unmitigated disaster most likely. I feel I have forgotten a large portion of the night's events, but luckily can still recall what day of the week it is. The word *Saturday* to the tune of Elton's 90s hit has been playing on a loop in my head all day.

I arrived early at the pub, only 'The Wassailers' were in attendance. Not an ideal name for the choir, very seasonal, but I assume the thinking behind it is they will not last all four of them. From what I could gather from the hoary throng, McKinney offered to buy a round at the bar some 30 minutes ago and had not yet returned. I assumed he had risked his life attempting to escape from the 70-foot upstairs toilet cubicle. The responsibility of acquiring the round then fell to me. However, I was forced, against my sweet will, to return empty-handed as the queue was horrifically long – well, aside from the drink Molly handed me. 'It's a Wetherspoons, not a sodding Soviet

Russia breadline, I'm sure they allow you to buy more than one drink,' piped up Sue of the tenor section, of all people (!) – who is in no position to comment on anything much, let alone Soviet Russia. A few sandwiches short of a picnic is Sue, a few faculties short of a university. Sue has been at the institute as a mature student since education began. I think she was raised in the Tudor Maze by urban foxes like a modern-day Romulus or Remus. I wouldn't be surprised if she was in fact part fox (she has been known to have violent outbursts over being denied surplus snake weights in the student library). I'm not sure of the moral acceptability of putting a woman in the tenor section when she is perhaps not 100 per cent able to consent to the arrangement, being the animal-human hybrid that she is. But it's Molly's gig and who wouldn't humbly consent to all of her demands. I would peaceably surrender a large portion of my brain to be under her baton for just one verse of 'Little Donkey'.

Despite my so-called 'gesture of festive ill will', aggravated by McKinney's blatantly toadying one of supplying all members with whisky sours, the choir soon managed to stir their hearts to produce a rapacious, bowel-rupturing rendition of 'Here We Come A-Wassailing', with Cudjoe shaking the tin in a very haphazard fashion. I disappeared to the cubicle in the sky for a moment, where I bumped into Wendy emerging. 'Why aren't you outside?' I said. Meaning, why are you here?!

'There's a big queue outside,' she said. I hoped she was not planning on urinating in the street again. She was wearing fingerless gloves and clutching her fingers in a peculiar manner, like a pardoner extracting his rings for resale. I hastened back down to the hellish gallows of the pub. I bumped into Molly on the narrow staircase, she smelt like almonds and roses. I felt a wisp of her hair brush against my forehead, which thrilled me to the core, as we squeezed past each other in the pitch-black dark. Wendy had cast a long and wide shadow from the top of the stairs.

She told me she had something to tell me, but the karaoke had started so I had an excuse to break away. It was like one of those moments in a Jane Austen film adaptation where it's announced that the dancing has started and the lovers are forced to separate – if the lovers were Mr Knightley and the unsightly weekend gardener, confined to the conifers, because his hands are too clumsy to care for the Campanula latifolia. I do care about Wendy, but she is well and truly a thorn in my side – a prickle in my pineal gland. Historically, she hasn't taken very much care with my conifer either.

Sandra Peacock had taken up the mic in the little booth, kicking off proceedings with a rendition of 'Scooby Snacks' by Fun Lovin' Criminals. The spoken introduction was performed by a woman waiting in the bar queue, although only the words 'fucking move' were audible over the din. Sandra was barely two minutes in before an alcohol-infused Wendy seized the microphone and requested 'My Way'. At which point an equally inebriated vicar in patent leather chaps stumbled into the booth and demanded a duet.

It transpired that our booth had been double booked along with a 'Tarts and Vicars' themed stag party. However, Wendy was unfazed by the intrusion. 'Bat Out of Hell' was selected on the machine. Once they'd untangled the microphone wires from the vicar's chain mesh leash, the performance went off without a hitch. Disappointingly for Wendy, I think she would've liked to take him home to meet the parents.

I stood with a tart at a safe distance a metre or two outside the booth – praying Molly wouldn't guess Wendy and I were acquainted. Disturbingly, not far enough away to see the next scene unfold. As they approached the final meaty cadenzas, Wendy began to peel away her bandages and wrapped her fingers suggestively and deliberately around the microphone stand, revealing the letters O A P P on the right hand and Y L O N on the left. 'Ay,' said the tart at my side. 'OAP Pylon – is that a sexual thing, I don't fancy that – I see enough of that at the care home!' Sadly, not even 'London's Most Glamorous and Promiscuous

Healthcare Assistant', as his sash said, could save us from the casualties of this night. The letters were so small as to be barely perceptible, unlike Wendy's unfortunately, which were clearly visible on her sizeable fingers – by myself, the room and Molly, who was approaching behind me with a couple of Woo Woos. Finally, the song ended, and Wendy began to re-wrap the offending digits, like a boxer preparing to don his gloves – but the killer blow had already been dealt. She gave Molly a thumbs up with her left hand, embossed with the letter N. The other hand bearing the letters HOAPP (an alternative spelling of 'hope' perhaps – I did not enquire further) she struggled to wrap left-handedly and kept hidden behind her back. Probably intentionally, it must be an error.

Molly pressed the Woo Woo into my chest without waiting for me to have hold of it. The second one she sent hurtling along the bar, where it landed in a research fellow's lap, seated at the other end. He spent the remainder of the night looking like a Smurf who had pissed himself. She mounted the bar. The vicar tripped in his haste to get a better view, severing the cable from the machine. '*Surabaya Johnny,*' she growled through an alcopop-coated larynx. '*Surabaya Johnny,*' she called out again, in an unhinged cabaret belt, which echoed in the palpable silence. Cudjoe scuttled to the piano. She sang the whole song in German, except the name Johnny of course. It was the most humiliating and excessively sexy thing I have ever experienced.

She disappeared into the night after that. I tried to catch up with her, but she'd already changed into her trainers. One day I swear I will catch up with her and walk or run by her side forever. I swear to love Molly Beaujolais 'til the day I die. I thank the Lord for bodged tattoos and poorly put together pub quizzes and red wine stains. Her name is a red wine stain on my heart. She is the embodiment of Beaujolais. Irremovable and always more costly than you anticipate.

December 15th – Dr Jonathan Nylon

It turns out Friday night was only phase one in the Great Unmitigated Disaster of 2019. Phase two rolled out this morning. The day had a cheerful start – campus is looking very festive; the trees are now decorated with fairy lights as well as toilet roll. The students had their Christmas party last night. I rolled my eyes at a group of students giggling at the improvised paper chains blowing like festival flags, but it did not instil the same level of fear as it did when Attila the Hun did it. Apparently, he was a right regular eye roller. He also claimed to have the sword of Mars in his possession. How did he get that through customs? Mind you, I've seen some hefty daggers passed over airport barriers, between staff and holidaymakers who can't get their stuff in the little plastic bags fast enough. I scaled the clock tower to get a better vantage point to view the carnage below, like the unpopular King Nabonidus surveying his war-torn kingdom from his siege tower. I climbed to the highest point (an attempt to escape from my existence perhaps?) and peered recklessly over the edge. The sight that greeted me, together with the self-imposed vertigo, caused me to chunder. The words 'Beaujolais is beau' were emblazoned in white below – as white as the white of Attila's rolling eyeballs. Oh God, it all came flooding back – the memories and the remains of the night's kebab lying dormant in my stomach. It was imprudent to aim for the ground below with so many students milling about, but I was thinking it would burn up like the speeding tail of a comet. Bailey's vomit however does not abide by the same laws of physics.

'There, where I have passed, the grass will never grow gain.'

December 15th – Dr Molly Beaujolais

I have just seen Johnny from my office window, hurling from the clock tower onto some students below. I cannot believe I kissed that man and declared my love for him only days previous. He better not follow me to New York. He will not be a 'living boy' there if he does.

December 16th – Dr Jonathan Nylon

Luce called me to say that Molly is travelling to New York, they're spending Christmas together there. She also told me 'to expect Bobby at midnight'. I would've cast him as the 'grasping, scraping, clutching, covetous old sinner' rather than one of the ghosts. Although he has the perfect face for the 'undigested bit of beef'.

1 am – no sign of Bobby.

December 17th – Dr Molly Beaujolais

I have been reflecting on Johnny and Vincent and what went wrong, why Johnny has sought out solace in the arms of a tar barrel-wielding usherette and why Vincent has found respite in exposing himself to other women on the internet. I'm not sure why. They're not sitting about thinking about me – they're hanging from the ceiling, like vampires.

I think the trouble I have with men is I give
them the impression I am wild and glamorous, but
really if you peel back the layers – deconstruct the
Russian doll, there is a wizened and jaded geriatric
figure inside – much like the Wizard of Oz. Perhaps
there has been some mistake in Vincent's case.

Perhaps there is another man walking around with
Vincent's penis, dismembered from his body and
wrapped up like a saveloy in a paper bag and string.
No, I hope not – I don't want any Mexican children
being disturbed.

Talking about children being disturbed, Nan
has been up to her old tricks again – terrorising the
locals. She is currently residing in the town of
Neumarkt, Lower Austria. It has been a non-stop
"orgy of Epicurean delights" apparently. Last night she
took a break from all the "drunken debauchery" to
indulge in a bit of festive pomp and ceremony. Her
friend Frieda invited her to a carol service at her local
church. Having been informed that the dress code was
fun, but informal, Nan arrived in a full Krampus
costume – unaware that half the children in attendance

suffer from Krampus-related PTSD. Once the "bleeding racket" (the cries, shouts and 'mutterings') had died down, Nan was relegated to the church kitchen to serve tea – the obstructive barrier of the counter being the crucial element in soothing the children's frayed nerves. Nan deemed it sensible, at this point, to remove her demonic Krampus head. However, upon removing it, the extremely lifelike 'lolling tongue', constructed out of molding clay and luncheon meat fell into the tea urn and immediately disintegrated, like a lost limb of the damned fizzling to nothing in the turgid waters of the river Styx. 'The children had to drink mulled wine and spiced whisky after that,' she concluded. I'm not sure why water or squash wasn't available. These things are never explained.

December 18th – Dr Jonathan Nylon

I forgot about the old folks Christmas dinner on Sunday. Received a poisoned pen from Margot this morning through the letter box, spotted with gravy and dripping in vitriol. I've been busy trying to prepare a 'nut-free' nut roast all day. They are descending en masse at 6 pm this evening. I was still clutching the letter and a blazing hot Pyrex dish when I glimpsed Bobby advancing up the street. I have never seen a man walk so slowly; it was worse than rush hour on the Central line. People were gesticulating wildly around him, but he didn't seem to notice. He moved like some kind of primordial beast – a throwback to *The Land Before Time*. Thank God I had Molly's apron and oven gloves on, I would've needed a trip to A&E otherwise – not being able to tear myself away from the extended scene.

I've set him up in the 'clown suite'. He's been in there for several hours now.

11 pm – finally, they've all vacated the premises – except Bobby of course. I think it would take him several months to do so. Good God, the slowness of the man! It's exasperating! I think it must be down to

all the ketamine he takes; I spotted a stash openly displayed for all the unworldly knick-knacks to behold when I was bringing him some towels. I was hoping he would stay put in the clown suite, like a self-excluding, surly teenager, but the elders badgered me to summon him down. Sometimes it is good for another person to enter the room when a couple are engaged in a heated row, it diffuses the tension. In this instance Eunice and Terry had found themselves at loggerheads over turning up to the occasion in allegedly the "exact same outfit". Terry protested of course, saying that his spattered smock was decorated with tomato ketchup and not a pointillist design of a Berlin brothel inspired by Seurat. I'm not sure how accurate a depiction it was of the scene described, but it certainly bore a resemblance to the dinner that was placed in front of us. I counted three globules of gravy on my plate – one was very raised like the hump of Bryn Celli Ddu. Similar to the burial site, it had encased within it ancient remains – undissolved granules from 1985 (I checked the tub after they left). Too little too late. I'm sure archaeologists will be discovering these mummified 'treasures' inside me in hundreds of years to come – my bowels are as blocked as the Neanderthals' evolutionary path.

Much like Neanderthal man, Bobby ultimately added nothing to the homo sapiens party. However, his silence still managed to inflict considerable confusion and distress. He spent the entire meal staring directly at Margot, who had adorned her face in a generous coating of rouge and blue eyeshadow and a circusesque red lip. She eventually said to him, 'Don't you know what I look like yet?' which Bobby misheard as, 'Don't you want to know what I look like yet?' The words prompted him to reach out a hand to touch Margot's face, which he did in a fumbling manner, squinting slightly. He later explained that he thought that she was trying to communicate that she was blind and wanted him to know what she looked like. The logic here is obviously lacking and we shall never know the full thought process that went on. I have heard that ketamine makes you forget things – but which senses are at your disposal is surely not on that list.

After Margot had been placated and moved to another seat, the evening seemed to go fairly smoothly. Bobby was relegated to the peripherals of the conversation, after being at the heart of things at the beginning of the meal: the oldies tried to include him by asking him to choose a prayer for grace. In haste, he chose the song 'Where's Your Mama Gone?' (Chirpy chirpy cheep cheep) perhaps inspired by the baby chicks on Eunice's fleece more than divine inspiration. Everyone politely obliged – Terry insisted we hold hands, which I deeply resented, it being flu season. I was overruled. We remembered nothing of the verses but still managed to keep the charade going for the full three minutes of the song. At least the food was sufficiently blessed, or spiritually bound by a cursus you could say.

December 19th – Dr Molly Beaujolais

Finally in NYC, but I've had to sell my soul to an aged devil to get here. His name is Professor Ralph Sotheby, and he is an art dealer. I think this is highly unlikely given his name, surely. He does have a face like a Picasso.

I was robbed – of a life among the stars for one – and also of my wallet, passport etc. at the departure lounge. That's where I met Ralph, slathering over a frothy coffee. He looked up at me with a smile that was less Hollywood red carpet, more Holyrood staff party post referendum results day – very lopsided. I would've preferred a wet weekend in Edinburgh to the regular downpour of saliva I was treated to during our conversation.

We rubbed shoulders in the Pret queue. I was hoping to scavenge a freebie but managed to acquire a human Furby instead. He seems to require constant attention and is a very slow yet frequent blinker. Anyhow, despite his many foibles he has promised to pay for my flight and accommodation, the only condition is that I share a few 'moments' with him, try not to throw him in front of a big yellow taxi etc. and point him in the direction of Bonhams on arrival. Disloyal to his namesake, he has his arthritic fingers in all the auction house pies it seems!

Conversation with him is excruciating. And at times unnerving – he threatened to stop off at his remote holiday castle in the Carpathian Mountains en route – luckily only direct flights were available. The mention of the medieval wine cellar piqued my interest, however. He has me under lock and key already.

December 20th – Dr Jonathan Nylon

I am the only person left on campus for the Christmas holidays – like Harry Potter, without the fame and adulation. I have acquired some of his academic disinclination of late. I've been asked to run a module on the Georgians – an historical epoch I have little to no interest in. Talking of people who would have no qualms in skinning a mouse's fur and applying it to bare skin, Wendy is the new university librarian now!

How she got the job, I don't know. She shows little

regard for the Dewey Decimal System – I've caught

her barrel-tossing books into the re-shelving bin on
many an occasion.

Still no word from Molly, I am very concerned. Luce
is not returning my calls, not since she deposited
Bobby. I have been in touch with the US Embassy but
received no reply. They must all be glued to the
presidential debates. Perhaps I can arrange a trade for
Bobby, when they get a moment – no, it'd never work
– he'd never pass the drug test.

December 21st – Dr Molly Beaujolais

I'm holed up in Ralph's hovel. He has a shrine to

Prince built into the wall. He says it came with the flat.
The rest is similarly decadent.

We ventured out this afternoon to find an
internet cafe. It was horrible. I managed to make
contact with Luce and relatives via Facebook however

– she has bought me an old Nokia phone, one with the buttons that give you repetitive strain. I'll donate it to Sotheby once I can upgrade. His joints are already shot. His attempt to direct the mouse was quite a sight to behold. Every time he needed to use it, he'd raise

his hand and let it fall from a great height, using gravity as a propellant – like a gull swooping to snatch a burger bun from the beach. The motion is completely ridiculous and causes the cursor to move out of sight and the mouse to move from the mat. He is like a child that makes annoying noises just for the sake of being annoying. I think there are bones of contention forming – metaphorical ones alongside his grinding brittle ones.

I am desperate to hear Johnny's voice, but I don't want to have to speak to him to hear it. The rantings of a young madman would be a welcome reprieve, as opposed to the frail whimperings of a deranged old one.

December 23rd – Dr Molly Beaujolais

Need to shake off Sotheby. But I ought to find an enclosed space to abandon him in – the weather is so bitterly cold. Went for a stroll in Central Park today, I had to wear three coats – purchased by Sotheby from Macy's. There was a collection of mounted policemen by the bins. I admired the chestnut and Sotheby insisted that I have a ride. I stressed that they are not for hire like donkeys on Weston-Super-Mare beach, but he would not hear it. He approached the horse and its dutiful rider and named his price. The bobbies did not turn round to greet the barterer. In fact, one kicked back a bit, the horse, not one of the policemen – causing him to drop his coins in the dust. I said, 'leave them, as antiques for your successors,' and he seemed to latch onto this romantic imagining. The notion may have even moved him somewhat, I think I saw him wipe a single tear from his watery cataract-ridden eye along with the dust that had made its way in there. It was a bold move, and I admired his grit in some respects. Unlike the horse, who clearly thought he needed some more of it.

3 pm – had lunch with Ralph at one of those restaurants with caricatures on the walls. I drew one of him, and the staff put it up in the window after we left – like a wanted poster. I turned around to view my handy work from the street after we left. With the sepia leopard print stockinged legs of the lady sitting in the window and a vase of fake flowers directly underneath it, the assemblage of parts resembled a life size *cadavre exquis,* exquisite corpse. A non-traditional one of course – usually only animal and human parts are permitted, this one was an atypical combination of vegetable, mineral and animal.

December 23rd – Dr Jonathan Nylon

Made contact with Molly. Well, that is not strictly true – I've made contact with some bizarre old man, claiming to be an associate of hers who answered the phone with 'Sotheby'. He is some kind of self-appointed 'minder'. What the hell is going on?! Molly mentioned that the Murano clowns are valuable items, are they in fact so priceless that she requires a 24/7 bodyguard from one of New York's most prestigious auction houses?

The poor man sounded very distressed. He launched into some surreal tale about ordering a steak and salad. He had specifically requested that the steak be served 'on the side'. When it arrived, it was presented on the plate – when he tried to protest to the waiter, Molly removed the steak from the plate with her fork and set it down upon the table next to the plate. I said, 'oh gosh, what happened next?' At which point Molly seized the phone and answered, 'He said thank you and ate it,' and hung up. Where has the sweet Brouwereseque maiden that I fell in love with gone?

December 24th – Dr Molly Beaujolais

I have just spent my Christmas Eve evening trapped in a box with the love child of Marcel Marceau and Basil Brush. No, I jest - Marcel Marceau would let you out after his routine was over. Sotheby had booked us a box at Le Scandal Cabaret and donned a black cape and white gloves for the occasion. The show was appalling.

I'm not sure if those characters would be able to forge a love child, but anything goes with Sotheby. And science is advancing every day, as is my conviction that he is the first living example of an alien birth. In the dim theatre lights, he was even more grotesque -- face half shrouded by the velvet drapes, Professor Ralph Sotheby, the Phantom of Ephemera.

I took my leave of him in the interval and went off in search of the facilities. The door I entered did not lead to the toilet, despite it having all the obvious signs of a lavatory (a laminated stick drawing of a woman pinned to it). It was the dressing room of the Liza Minelli impersonator.

'Can you help me fix my curl baby ... just a dab.' She gestured to a pot of boot polish with an inch long peach talon. 'It gets under my manicure,' she said.

'You ok hunny? Man trouble?'

'Oh no,' I said. 'He's not my man, he's my grandfather.' She raised a lacquered eyebrow.

'That man got you fitted up, but does he fit on you? He gotta fit on you, snug, like a fox fur stole, baby girl. If his shoes don't fit, don't wear them – let someone else feel the benefit of them. I gave a pair of Hollister diamanté stilettos to a homeless man just last week – they don't fit no more hunny, get rid. Someone else will appreciate them.'

I was desperate to ask how a pair of shoes could no longer fit anymore – what had changed the shoes or the size of her feet? But I held my tongue, she was sitting still with her eyes closed and looked as if she was done – I noticed she had three rows of eyelashes. America truly is the land of abundance. A call for beginners crackled over the Tannoy.

I added a final slick to her baby doll curl and zipped up her sequin gown. Her eyes sparkled in the gloom.

'You gotta do your own growing baby.'

The feet then.

11.30 pm – Sotheby has gone to the Carpathians to see his "Little Prince". I don't know whether this is his son, his lover or a hallucination – he didn't say.

1.30 am– just remembered that I left Johnny a Christmas and birthday present in his office on Friday – hopefully he won't discover them. I hid them under a stack of lurid billets-doux in his drawer, God knows who they were from! Wrapped in a plastic wallet like police evidence, they didn't look like they'd been lovingly handled too often.

December 24th – Dr Jonathan Nylon

I can't afford a flight out to New York, but I am
desperate to see Molly. I've been sat here playing with
an empty packet of Tayto chips, like James when he is
stuck in his room, dreaming of riding away to a better
life on a peach. How can I adequately convey to her
that I have barrel-tossed Wendy aside? It's Christmas
Eve, a time to be with loved ones and I am in my
office – missing her. Need to start driving home, but I
can't move. Just opened my drawer and there are two
gifts from her, one for Christmas and one for birthday:
a signed and framed photo of slave Leia in her gold
bikini and a miniature Bingo game. I would give my
right and/or left arm to play a game of Bingo with her
right now, just the two of us – all cosy in my office. I
know that may cause some practical issues with playing
the game at first, but it would be worth it. I would go
to any length to make her happy – she could always be
in charge of the little red felt tip if needs be.

December 25th – Dr Molly Beaujolais

Called Mum and we reminisced about Dad – how he would always buy us a Corgi car, as an investment piece for Christmas and birthdays. And the year he asked us to guess which one in his collection was the least, and the most expensive. The winner was awarded the toy, the loser had to listen to Dad talking at length about the Corgis – there was one winner, but we were all losers. I am to this day the proud owner of his pre-WW2 Crescent battleship, complete with sailors. I picked it because I wanted to be an oil tank driver's wife when I grew up. I was nine. Later, I went down to the harbour to watch the boats. Luce and I had had our Christmas lunch at 'New York's most romantic restaurant' and I saved some of the cracker paper. I made a boat and set it upon the water. Merry Christmas, Saint Nick Beaujolais.

December 25th – Dr Jonathan Nylon

So, this is Christmas and what have you done? Been laid out like a trauma patient for most of it. My mother is not in a good way – she bit into a Christingle sweet

295

last night and lost a crowned tooth to it. The bartender discovered it on the floor just in time apparently, the pub dog was advancing on it. I wonder if Molly is lazing about in her dressing gown somewhere – probably a silk one worn by a pre-Raphaelite nude, donated by Sotheby's. I imagine she is reclining on a chaise lounge in some swanky apartment, like Kate Winslet in *Titanic*, surrounded by a handpicked selection of Sotheby's finest. Is it alright to think about sex on Jesus' birthday? I think the detail of me anointing her in Frankincense and essential oils might be a bit much?

Should I call her again? When are they going to invent a diary that can talk back? I'll have to start communicating with Siri on a regular basis, rather than a blank page. All these unanswered questions, it's giving me flashbacks to my days as a zealous altar boy.

December 26th – Dr Molly Beaujolais

Vincent is here. And Sotheby is back already. He claims that the catfishing behaviour was research for an art project – he showed me the pictures from the exhibition, but they were very blurry. He really needs to invest in a digital camera. I made him a coffee anyhow, only instant – no expense or effort spared.

Bobby told him everything, unaware that we'd broken up – he saw my address on a bit of paper left out on a "spare inch of kitchen surface". Glad to hear he's keeping the place tidy, good God. Give people an inch – they'll invite your ruinous ex back into your life. My feelings are all over the place – as are my possessions. Vincent does not approve of the Sotheby set-up.

'You need someone more arty,' he said.

'Why does everyone assume I'm in a relationship with this ancient man!'

'You are living with him, Molly.'

'Yes, but like a carer, like someone in one of those help-the-aged schemes.'

At that moment a whimpering sound could be heard emanating from the bathroom. I explained that the apartment is very old, and the door gets stuck sometimes. 'Good God, Molly,' he purred (Vincent, not Ralph – Ralph had fallen silent by this point).

8 pm – I've sent Vincent packing. Ralph and I are going to paint the town red like Zelda and Scott – a taste of Gatsby living before we reach *The Crack-Up*.

December 26th – Dr Jonathan Nylon

I called Molly. Vincent answered and told me to fuck off. Don't really feel like writing.

December 27th – Dr Molly Beaujolais

I think I have perhaps done a terrible thing. I promised to take Sotheby to Bonhams, but I left him at the subway. I let him get on the train and stayed put on the platform as the doors slowly closed in front of his bemused face, I was frozen to the spot. It was like *Sliding Doors* without the whimsical, romantic subplot.

It's not surprising I couldn't help my students; I can't

even help an old man off a train. I tried to better myself by relocating to the 'Land of the Free' and all I have liberated is a confused geriatric into the wild urban jungle of NYC. It will be better this way.

10 pm – Called Johnny. He didn't answer. Better find myself a new darling then. Out of all the people, in all the subways, in all the world, I'll never walk past one like Johnny.

December 27th – Dr Jonathan Nylon

I've been keeping myself busy, building a Sylvanian empire. My sister has thankfully left me in charge of Tilly all day. I keep subconsciously engineering scenes where lonesome characters end up in a state of distress and require a comforting hug from another animal. It's like some bizarre kind of play therapy. She is not the most sympathetic of counsellors. The poor hedgehog mother has been abandoned face down mid-ice-skating party, probably blubbing uncontrollably into an icy pond – while Tilly's busy dancing to the *Trolls*

Christmas Special. Why do I have so many cold and callous women in my life?

December 28th – Dr Molly Beaujolais

Went to see *Cats* at the cinema with Luce. Being in the company of Grizabella for an hour and fifty minutes reminded me of times spent trapped with a pub stranger who wants to tell you their life story. I felt sorry for her at the end though when she was taken up into the sky in a hot-air balloon. She thought she was getting a no-expense-spared stay at the luxury Heaviside Layer, not an Icarus- style death!

December 29th – Dr Jonathan Nylon

Back in Maida Vale. Bobby and I are watching Oliver!

– he's never seen it. Can't stop thinking about Molly -

all these Cockney characters aren't helping the situation. That scene where Ron Moody pulls out a seemingly never-ending stream of multi-coloured

handkerchiefs, I've seen her do that with a pack
of Kleenex during the Vincent days. She's so wasteful.

I found Bobby in his room, staring at the clowns again
– sitting very still on the edge of the bed. I made him a
roast dinner, I'm not sure he's been eating properly.

He was wearing Molly's pink dressing gown and
looked very wan. We got into a discussion about
musicals. It turns out he is a big fan – 'Being Alive'
from Sondheim's *Company* is a particular favourite of
his, *Someone to hold me too close. Someone to hurt
me too deep,*' he sang. '*Someone to spit in my chair.*'

 'Sit,' I corrected him.

 'Ah right. Yeah, I did think that was a bit odd.'

 I suppose it does make sense with the following
'someone to ruin your sleep' line. Bobby wouldn't
require human assistance there, he has the clowns for
that.

 He is growing on me. Although his living habits
still leave something to be desired. Tilly gave me
alphabet fridge magnets for Xmas, so I have been

leaving helpful instructions for him with them – like 'wash'. Hopefully it will help.

I have sacrificed the letters for 'lock the door' and gaffer-taped these to the door frame.

December 30th – Dr Molly Beaujolais

Luce and I joined the Hasidic Jews marching in Monsey today, in solidarity with the Hanukkah celebrants and those wounded in the Saturday attack. We were invited back to five different families' houses for a full festal meal, but politely declined. I am resolving to not impose on others' hospitality from henceforth.

December 31st – Dr Jonathan Nylon

I am concerned for Molly with all the tensions festering in the US at the moment, following the Iraq airstrikes. Flaming torches and shouts of 'Death to

America' outside the U.S Embassy in Baghdad reported today – not that Molly could ever be mistaken for a Republican or even an Americanophile – she boycotts all US sitcoms and won't even enter a Starbucks. Trump is not exactly treading lightly over the tightrope of international negotiations with tweets such as: 'They will pay a very **BIG PRICE!** This is not a Warning, it is a Threat. Happy New Year!' Reminds me of my interactions with Bobby in some respects, his latest habit is leaving the door unlocked on a regular basis. After several discussions, I decided to venture a comical yet, I hope, authoritative note today, wrapped around Catchpole's pole: 'Please remember to lock the door, otherwise my brothers and I may have to be sold into prostitution or, to a travelling circus troupe of ill repute to pay for the damages. We would miss you terribly. Seasons' Greetings! The Clowns in Your Room.'

January 1st, 2020 – Dr Molly Beaujolais

I met a man in a bar last night who is designing an app to aid with calculating votes at the forthcoming caucuses. The first will be in Iowa in February 2020. He decided there and then that he was in love with me, and he was going to incorporate my initials into the coding somehow. I think it will be one of the most romantic gestures anyone has performed for me. He said I have derailed him like a subway train, which doesn't quite work as an analogy for everlasting love, a subway or any other kind of train for that matter wouldn't have far to go if it were derailed. Our future in fact lasted one more hour after that, and we voyaged only as far as the neighbouring speakeasy. He got blind drunk on Old Fashioneds and passed out on a powder-blue, velour couch. His friend was very concerned about him; he said he needs to be up early tomorrow to begin programming for the app. I wrote my initials on his hand in case he forgot, but not my number.

January 2nd – Dr Jonathan Nylon

New Year's Eve spent watching the *Hootenanny* with a comatose Bobby in his pants is not what I would describe as a positive omen for the year ahead. Stormzy performed a track from his new album *Heavy is the Head*. Has he also spent three hours straight on a sofa with Bobby? He was asleep on me within half an hour, I didn't know you could get a 'dead shoulder'.

10 pm – Bobby is still leaving the door open, ajar even! Returned to my note, crossed out the bit about prostitution and circus troupes and replaced it with: 'will stay forever – have loud sex and multiply and form complex civilisations that will be hard to shift.'

1 am – door is locked and double-bolted.

January 3rd – Dr Molly Beaujolais

Luce and I have relocated to a hotel themed on the Titanic. We sank a few mojitos this morning to celebrate. Our stay here will be short – Luce has been

offered a prop-making job for a new 'zombie live

action video game experience' in Boise, Idaho. She

says they are looking for box office staff. It looks like

this American dream I am living will morph into a

dystopian nightmare before I make my return journey.

January 4th – Dr Jonathan Nylon

I'm not enjoying preparing for my lectures on 'The

Georgians'. It turns out they are a bunch of dullards –

the rumours that George I was a sexual deviant were

unfounded and spread by a xenophobic courtier called

Lord Chesterfield. According to Philip, George

rejected no woman so long as she was 'very willing,

very fat and had great breasts'. I see a lot of myself in

George I, and I can't say I'm happy about it.

January 4th – Dr Molly Beaujolais

There is a lot of sex on the menu at the moment, but I am perusing it with all with a glassy-eyed detachment – I wish Johnny would talk to me. Flicking through a sea of dating app souls, endlessly swiping left, I keep feeling compelled to say all their names in my head for some reason, like a roll call of lost WW1 soldiers. I am applying the Nigella Lawson 'imagine yourself eating it' rule to see what I want, but when the course is served, I don't seem to be getting much enjoyment from the helping dished out. I often have to help myself afterwards in fact. I'm surprised so many men are able to perform with the cold expression of a slayer looking back at them, well it worked for the clients of Phil Spector – I hope this is not the face I am presenting to the world. A man asked me to put my hands on his face the other day during sex – which I think was unfair, they were very occupied at the time – turning the pages of the *New Yorker*, but still.

January 5th – Dr Jonathan Nylon

I am so cut up about Molly. The pain has driven me back to Mother Nature – spent all day at the allotment today. She called me, but I can't talk to her – not knowing that Vincent is pawing her with his greasy oil-painted hands in the background. I confided in the old folks about my broken heart. They recommended I look forward to other things, like my dinner. I can't even do that – can't cook in the kitchen with Bobby mixing his Georgian tinctures in there: 2 parts nutmeg and sugar, 2 parts live bacteria and urine. It's not hygienic.

Managed to cobble together a lecture of sorts for the first episode of 'The Georgians'. They seem to be unpleasant and tedious in equal measures – with their blood sports and occasional peacemaking tendencies. I am tempted to just stick on some J. C. Bach and let a PowerPoint of pictures of pretty buildings play out – like a presentation of holiday snaps. It was a flourishing time for art and architecture.

Hopefully McKinney will walk in, assume I've lost the plot and fire me.

It seems highly unlikely he will be doing that any time soon unfortunately. He called me into his office today and confessed that he knows I am responsible for the 'Long Man of Wilmington' tribute on the campus lawn. However, I am a valued member of the faculty staff, and he is prepared to turn a blind eye. He then explained that Molly's been fired, for numerous reasons – mostly relating to her incompetence as a lecturer, but he finds it hard to believe she didn't have a hand in all this. Oh God. By attempting to make a dramatic entrance onto the stage of Molly's life, I have forced her to exit it. Our relationship and any hope for a future one has gone up in flames. My grand romantic gesture, intended to engender a special effect, has in actual fact caused an ill-timed pyrotechnic display, resulting in multiple casualties, skilfully and despicably concealed from the audience thanks to an overenthusiastic theatre technician's (McKinney's) insistence on the use of a smoke machine in every scene.

January 6th – Dr Molly Beaujolais

I've been Googling Boise – and it is actually a cultural hotspot. I'm getting quite excited about this new adventure now. There is the Gene Harris Jazz Festival, Boise Contemporary Theater, ComedySportz Boise, the Egyptian Theatre, Treefort Music and Idaho Shakespeare Festivals and Hewlett-Packard's offices. Perhaps I could even get a job at Boise State University. There is even an 'avant garde satirical tradition of puppetry for millennials', kept alive by HomeGrown Theatre, according to *Wikipedia.* We've missed the *Idaho Potato Bowl,* but we're still in time for *Jerry Seinfeld Live* at the Morrison Center.

January 7th – Dr Molly Beaujolais

We are yet to arrive in Boise. Because we're not going there. We're going to Peck – Idaho's most minute village. Population 186 – there are more than 25 times as many varieties of plant in Idaho than there are people in this place. It is 0.3 square miles big and has one 'small creek'. And one small prick – the manager, an eccentric man from Perth who wears individual toe socks and sandals; apparently, was unable to secure the building rights for a site based in Boise.

We are now on the last leg of our journey – a train to Orofino. We're going to hitch or walk from there. A group of snivelling Californian gap year students started chatting to us on the train. One was holding a punnet of grapes in a brown paper bag. They warned us to turn back as there is no work in Peck. I thanked the cold-ridden youngster for the advice, and he offered me a grape. I wanted to refuse, but he had a desperate look in his eye. I took one – it was bitter to the taste and would not dissolve on my tongue. Like rain on the unyielding Midwest earth.

January 8th – Dr Jonathan Nylon

I want to go home to Waterley Bottom, but I have back-to-back lectures all week and a meeting with Professor Lannister. She's been in the library a lot

lately, thank God. So has the student admirer. It's

been good to have someone to converse with as a means of escaping his penetrating gaze. My heart and mind are in agony over Molly. I feel like I've been

smashed over the head with a lapis lazuli, like Birkin in *Women in Love.* I think I need to feel some greenery between my fingertips. Perhaps I could strip naked and roll around the Tudor Maze for a bit to assuage

my pain. Don't think Sue would appreciate me brushing myself up against a bush next to the bench she likes to eat her sandwiches on though, what's left of them. She's more than a few short.

More research for lectures, I've left it to the last minute somewhat. If you hit a Georgian with a lapis lazuli paperweight, it would probably bounce straight back off, they were so thick skulled. I miss Molly so much, her and her pretty, delicate, clever skull.

January 9th – Dr Molly Beaujolais

We've arrived. We managed to hitch a ride with a family of six in a pickup truck (half the town). When we pulled up at the farm yesterday, the farmer was nowhere to be see. He eventually appeared from a cloud of dust, like an obscure *Stars in Their Eyes* contestant; perhaps the facilities manager, or some such character who has found his way into the spotlight, having served many arduous years by Matthew's side, waiting for his time to shine. The farmer's criss-crossed visage bore the scars of a chequered life lived in pain and struggle. I didn't share my 90s prime-time themed thoughts with him. I've

313

now been briefed on my box office duties – there is a clause in my contract which states that I have to plough the onion-laden land on the weekends. Our digs are next to the dig – a small cabin for two with a large cupboard for our 'tools' (a Smith and Wesson Dark Earth 6.5 Creedmoor rifle and a selection of Imacasa machetes).

January 10th – Dr Jonathan Nylon

Bobby is continuing to occupy the hall – he has now created a makeshift sofa/lounging space within the cupboard. How much misery can one man bear!

Meeting with Prof Lannister seemed to go alright – she enquired whether I am 'OK'. I mentioned the paper I am currently writing on medieval Cornish people (started today). I roped in the student admirer actually – just to create a bit of distance. I sent him off to the History section in the library and asked him to make some notes for me. He came back six hours later without a jot to show for himself. He said to me, 'It's not my fault nothing happened to Cornish people in medieval times.' Perhaps I will have to rethink my subject. I also let slip about Molly, she was very sympathetic. Invited me for a drink. I hope she can help me find a way through all this; I need to find a way to make amends for Molly's demise!

January 12th – Dr Jonathan Nylon

Actually, I'm convinced I'm paying for my sins already, in this life and the next simultaneously (a distant spiritual realm I am unable to reap the benefits from). I am living my worst past life alongside my present, in a presently far-from-best body. Bobby needs constant tending to. And I have taken on the life of a lowly courtier to satisfy his needs. I'm a servile shadow of my former self. I came home this afternoon, and he was only halfway down the stairs. I had to wait another 15 minutes with two heavy Waitrose shopping bags in hand before he'd completed his descent. I'm going to have to write to the council and ask them to have a stairlift fitted. It's infuriating.

No life for a young single man. This must be how the imperial envoy Zhang Qian felt – constantly

ferrying goods to the emperor and bringing news of the
Western world outside. Like the noble nomadic
Scythians, Bobby feels more spiritually at home
camped out in Kansu Corridor than luxuriating in the
alcázar of Genghis Khan. How can I get him to
relocate to his bedroom quarters? He is determined to
occupy the hallway.

His room has taken on the aroma of a herd of
steppe-reared steeds as well, which is making its way
out to the communal areas. My abode has the fresh
fragrance of the presidential palace of Ulaanbaatar in
comparison. If I could at least steer him towards
inhabiting an enclosed space, the enclave of the
Xinjiang region, rather than the entire steppe, that
would be a start. But unfortunately he insists on
keeping his borders open for business at all times. I
think he may be entamaphobic – I suppose he is
bringing a certain optimistic feeling back to this
household – one door closes and another one
immediately opens with Bobby.

11 pm – think I might start work on a paper on servant lives at the court of Genghis Khan, it will be imbued with lots of real emotion.

January 13th – Dr Molly Beaujolais

Walked seven miles in search of a tourist information centre. It turns out the nearest one is approximately 127 miles away, the waitress at the Canyon Cafe informed me. I stopped for a quick cup of coffee before embarking on the other 120. I saw nothing but onions and a man walking a horse on a rope with no saddle, like Tommy Shelby in *Peaky Blinders*. He had colourless hair, gelled into long spikes, not dissimilar to the wafting onion fronds. Perhaps I'll meet a similar vegetative fate. I found somewhere six fields in – it was closed, more than closed – six fields in and six feet under. There was someone inside, but there were also boards nailed to the windows, so I didn't press it, or them – they looked like they would give you a septic splinter and there isn't a hospital for miles around. I spotted a piece of paper on the floor by the bin outside, I picked it up for something to read later – out loud to Luce as we huddle in our freezing cabin. It was a call for correspondents to converse with death row-bound inmates of South Boise Prison Complex. 'You can make a difference' it said.

6.30 pm – called the number on the notice. I am being set up with a man named Joel Jericho Souris. I am not allowed to know his crime(s).

January 14th – Dr Jonathan Nylon

Class were very unruly today. I didn't handle it well. 'If we were in Georgian times and you didn't pay attention, someone might kidnap you and force you to join the Navy!' I said. 'Yes, please,' the student admirer piped up.' Threatening to tie him to a chair (like a Georgian physician would do as part and parcel of his medical practice) if he didn't desist was not the most well thought out of responses. He was particularly enthusiastic in his support of this idea – he probably has a fetish like

Beckett's *Murphy*. I'm pleased that somebody can still feel something resembling human feeling, even if they need the help of an inanimate object to achieve it.

8 pm – home at last. Popped into Farringdon Boots to pick up some conventional medicinal supplies (Bobby's home remedies will not suffice). The shop assistant took an age to serve me with a sales patter developed by Dynamo it seems, full of flourishes it was. I felt quite guilty, the show was worth more than the £1 tube of Colgate I effectively paid for it.

January 15th – Dr Molly Beaujolais

Drafted my first letter to Joel:

Dear Joel,

I hope this finds you well. I found the notice about South Boise Prison Complex inmates seeking amicable correspondence with civilians from the outside world on a church notice board and thought I'd reach out. I don't know where to start, life must be

319

unbearably hard for you, and I hope I can provide some comfort and larks perhaps. I've recently moved to Peck, Idaho, but I'm from Bermondsey in Southeast London originally – I work in the box office of a zombie attraction and plough an onion field on the weekends. I am living with my friend Luce in a cabin on site; she is an artist. I used to be a lecturer in Performing Arts and Applied Theatre, but I was fired. Well, resigned (it was a who can draw first sort of situation) for various reasons, none of which could be proved. So perhaps we have some things in common already. I am 28, I have red hair and hazel eyes. I would be very interested to hear about your days and please feel free to share your thoughts and concerns with me.

Very best wishes,

Dr Molly Beaujolais

I couldn't tell him I found it in the dirt next to a bin. I sent it via courier – not sure I trust the local postal service around here. Hopefully they will select the fastest unsaddled horse for me. I hope our correspondence will bring us both up in the world, up and on to a higher spiritual plane. Otherwise, I'm booking the first physical plane out of here.

January 17th – Dr Molly Beaujolais

Work has begun on the zombie apocalyptic set. The manager has made contact with me, via text – I've never met him. He's like that faceless character out of *Inspector Gadget.* He said I need to inform visitors that we are: 'the world's largest zombie zoo experience, 450 rooms, 230 floors.' Luce suggested I downscale it to "Europe". I said, 'we're not in Europe,' and she said, 'I know, it just feels more honest.' I don't know how I'm going to convince people there are 230 floors – you can see through the scaffolding there are only five.

January 18th – Dr Jonathan Nylon

Wendy informed me today that she found a letter addressed to me in the library comments box. She said she was surprised to find a comment in there that wasn't from me. Perhaps not so surprising since she banned me from posting any recently. She also informed me that she has struck up a romantic friendship with the vicar and will be having the tattoos on each finger covered with miniature dog collars They are going to see the Meatloaf musical *Anything for Love* at Scarborough Spa. I used to love that song, 'I Would Do Anything for Love', until someone at school told me it was about anal sex. I asked Wendy's

opinion on this theory, and she said, 'no, that can't

possibly be true – I know from first-hand experience.' I proffered my congratulations – for what exactly at that point, I'm not sure.

The letter is from my very own Elio Perlman of course. A poem, mad as the Macedonian Front. He makes an equally valiant albeit fundamentally flawed military-style effort. Unlike the Allied Forces coming to help the Serbs in World War 1, it's definitely a case of too much, too soon where he's concerned, rather than too little, too late.

Here's the poem:

I am jealous of your sheets,
Jealous of your suspender folders,
Jealous of your little red pen,
Making scratches on your diary page
 And rivets in my heart.
Jealous of your manhood
And all that you touch
And touches you on a regular basis

Well, he needn't be jealous – nothing will be touching me on a regular basis, because I'll be doing my bit to combat coronavirus, should it make its way to these shores.

8 pm – dropped into Boots on the way home and stocked up on toiletries to be on the safe side. He was there again. The shop assistant, not the admirer – he is worlds apart from that potentially murderous character, with his sweet Scottish serenade – although I'm sure he's lured a few sailors onto the rocks in his time, in a metaphorical sense (on a night out in Inverness no doubt!). I felt quite emotional when he asked me if I have a Boots card. I had nearly had a meltdown standing in front of Johnson's 'No More Tears' just moments before.

1 am – Just woken up from a dream involving the Boots assistant – he was mopping my brow with an iodine-soaked rag inside a hospital tent on the banks of the river Somme. He applied it tenderly at first, but then decided to dry cough into it and discard it with a Houdiniesque flourish over my bare torso and face. How has this man entered my subconscious mind? I need to spend less time contemplating the inner workings of a man who handles miniature bottles of shampoo all day and more time working on my paper.

No one knows how Genghis Khan died or where he's buried, so at least my fears won't be exacerbated with that morbid line of enquiry – that silken trail has gone cold, thank God.

January 19th – Dr Molly Beaujolais

Letter from Joel:

Molly, you sound like a hot piece of ass. Excuse my French. Do you speak French as well? You sound kind of fancy. Write soon. Joel x

P.S. What are larks?

January 20th – Dr Jonathan Nylon

Molly called me again. I was with Professor Lannister in my office. It's not how it sounds. Molly didn't see it that way.

There was a brief tussle – Lannister pinned me to the desk I confess, but I was an innocent bystander in many ways. She knocked the Laia picture onto the floor and it smashed. Beacon's poem fell out from the frame – signed, 'Love, Molly'.

January 21st – Dr Molly Beaujolais

Dear Joel,

Thank you for your sweet sentiments. It has been said I am a "hot piece of ass' as you put it, but it's impolite to self-declare these things. As it happens, I have nothing to declare, my heart is a shrivelled piece of coal and my mind is a barren wasteland – I used to be so creative, always writing poems and composing music. But I made the mistake of falling in love and now I am spiritually and creatively bankrupt. Larks – I wish I could tell you Joel, but I am not so sure these days. Do you like to create things? What are your hobbies? I'm very curious to know how you fill your days. Do you have a girlfriend or friends inside or out?

You seem like a romantic soul. I hope you don't mind me sharing, but I went through a romantic trauma of my own recently. The man I believed myself to be in love with, is in fact, shagging his professor. I called him and caught them in the act – he's still staying in my flat as well, well my Nan's flat – Tab Hunter donated it to her in 1966. I think you would like it; we have some William Morris originals in there and a beautiful collection of Murano clowns. Anyhow, I said, 'I hope you're not still squatting in my flat,' to which he said nothing. Well, life goes on – or plods on ... ploughs on! I hope you are keeping well.

Much love,
Dr Molly Beaujolais

I put it in the courier's hand myself and asked him to pass on the message. He kissed it before he passed it back to me, my hand that is, not the letter. Although he doesn't strike me as the most efficient envoy, the man has no bag nor a stitch of waterproof clothing to his name! Much like his unsaddled horse.

January 22nd – Dr Jonathan Nylon

I'm going to attempt to take on Molly's class – drastic
times require drastic measures. I keep seeing her
students about campus, why they haven't re-enrolled in
other classes or left the university I don't know. Re-
indoctrinated – they are moving about like lost lambs,
hungry to be sacrificed on the altar of poor education.
Perhaps I can convince McKinney to extend the
course and hire Molly again, if we can stage a half
decent version of the play they were preparing. It's
time I started challenging myself more.

With any luck it'll be like that film *Nativity!*
where the female protagonist returns from her
glamorous life in America to settle for Martin
Freeman.

I found them all by the campus recycling bins,
gathered around the carcass of the old vending
machine, singing the old songs like the tramp from *A
Clockwork Orange* or the down-and- out kids in that

Sondheim one where they live in a shopping mall –

Evening Primrose. Bobby's been making us watch a lot

of musical theatre lately. The new gun freshers

parading passed with a kind of vindictive enthusiasm.

One of the classmates was drinking a can of

Monster in a ripped brown paper bag. He drained the

dregs and crushed it in his left hand casting it aside.

'Let's get to work,' I said to them, coarsely and

authoritatively. After introducing myself and asking

him politely to put the can in the mixed recycling bin,

of course.

January 23rd – Dr Molly Beaujolais

Just finished clearing up after the 'friends and family

night' at Zomzooville. I think I still have boiled onion

in my hair. The farmer put on a hog roast – I was

standing in line waiting for my pork slider and

suddenly a strange whispering resounded in my left

ear, I could scarcely make it out over the buzzing of

flies. It made me jump out of my skin, I thought it was

the pig for a moment, but it was the manager –

creeping up from behind in his Hush Puppy sandals. He went in headfirst – he has quite a stooped stance. I felt the breath from his words before I heard them – the head brought low from the heaviness of all the malintent it's holding. He wished my left shoulder "good luck" and left before I could ask him my questions regarding payment, contractual Ts and Cs etc.

The 'friends and family night' was a horrifying occasion. The actors were in an absolute state after several punters had "gotten rowdy" – their own flesh and blood! One guest had apparently picked up a plastic meat cleaver and chanted 'die zombie slut', until a steward forcibly removed him. I shall be processing a lot of refunds tomorrow, no doubt.

January 24th – Dr Jonathan Nylon

I've booked my students in for a **trip** to the Globe, for inspiration – both classes. I am nervous about how my history students will react to these new 'alien' interlopers and whether they will take to them or not. I'm not sure I've taken to any of my students to be

perfectly honest, I don't know any of their names in fact! I am more familiar with the student admirer than I'd like to be of course – he sidled past me in a pair of very tight corduroy trousers in the Recreation section of the student library the other day. A very harrowing experience. I wish I was as well acquainted with his coursework as I now am with his genitals. I'm going to have to start using the public library.

January 25th – Dr Molly Beaujolais

Spoke to Nan and told her all about Joel, the overfamiliar mounted courier and various members of the living dead contingent. She is intrigued, but ultimately concerned and wants me to fly back to Blighty immediately. I'm the one who should be concerned! She is planning on participating in a nude calendar to raise money for the Australian bushfire cause. Her and 'Boy' are going to squirrel away some of the funds to pay for my flight. The title of the calendar will be *Sizzling Septuagenarians*, I suggested that this might not be the most sensitive of titles given the number of lives going up in flames – literally in the case of the marsupials. She said she is doing her bit for the little creatures and sent me a picture via text of her posing with a man who seemed to be wearing a hair shirt (Boy?). He was holding a banner saying

'COMFORT OUR KOALAS'. 'I've adopted one,' she said. 'I can see that,' I said, relegating the snap of the fur coated bush baby to my deleted items folder.

January 26th – Dr Jonathan Nylon

Tried calling Molly, but I can't get through. Bobby

gave me her Nan's number and I gave her a call.

There was a lot of distress and confusion at first as I tried to reassure her that I have never been to Boise or killed a man. It was eventually revealed that Molly has been corresponding with a Midwest convict, who rides an unsaddled horse and Ivy suspects "it is love".

Passed the Wormwood Scrubs correctional facility on my way home from campus. Several horrifying scenes involving Molly and inmates flashed through my mind. I have learnt from numerous TV dramas that the canteen is often the location for the most dramatic scenes of prison life. I imagined my sweet Beaujo having her russet hair and pretty face thrust into a plate of putrid pie and mash. She would never survive it, she has very refined culinary tastes.

January 27th – Dr Molly Beaujolais

Letter from Joel:

Molly, I sure am sorry to hear about your misfortunes. I knew a girl whose guy went off with another guy as well once, she was real cut up about it too. Maybe he is immature – he must be young if he has a prof. You sound like the kind of woman who would need the love of a real man. Morris and Murano clowns, I don't

*know what those things are, but they sound pretty, and
I can picture you lying out in one of them fields of
cornflower – now that is a pretty picture. Hang that
one on the wall if I had one. As it happens, I have
plenty of walls about me, but no pictures to hang. My
days are kind of samey, sugar tits. I get up and wait to
die like any other man. Tell me more about your day!
I bet you and sweet Lucy Lu are looking forward to
catching some rays in the onion field come spring. I
would like to see your onions Molly, but I think it is
impolite to declare. Write soon. Joel x*

Scribbled my RSVP on a potato chip packet and
delivered to the courier.

Dearest Joel,

*Things are OK here on the farm. Luce and I are
enjoying lots of cosy nights in. The ploughing work is
hard and time spent in the box office soul-destroying,
but we are keeping cheerful with games of Rummy and
bottles of gin. We're thinking about going on a road*

trip soon, not far – maybe just to Ketchum and back.
I've heard there is a Tourist Information Centre there.

Write soon. Molly x

I'm starting to wonder whether this courier is legit.

His prices keep going up. I don't care, he does the job

and many more besides. I've seen him flipping burgers

in the kitchen at Canyon café, when he's not roaming
with his steed. He offered to help fix the box office
software last time I was in as well. He's going to take a
look next week, I couldn't say no – my disclosure
agreement forbade me from revealing it's not the
technology's fault the prices are so wrong.

January 28th – Dr Jonathan Nylon

Gathered the drama class for our first session in the
underground bunker classroom. What they lack in
dramatic ability, they certainly make up for in

enthusiasm and volume. Poggio, in particular, could've

resurrected Pongo and friends from the Disney

archives with his high-pitched caterwauling. The plot is extremely confusing, but I think we can make it work if we ply the audience with enough alcohol.

January 29th – Dr Molly Beaujolais

Another day in Box Office Bedlam. I think I have my sales patter down to a T at least. It begins with 'this is Europe's largest live action video game experience' (as prescribed) and ends with me repeating the word 'bye' in quick succession until they exit the booth. The town's curiosity about the attraction is insatiable, I have had to hide under the desk on several occasions today. The actors are getting on my nerves as well. I've never known a group of human beings to take such an active interest in the minutiae of box office daily affairs. They want to know everything and regularly subject me to a full Spanish-style inquisition: 'What is this?' (A: a pen) Q: 'What is that?' (A: a glowstick) and they insist on touching everything on the desk. 'How many tickets have we sold?' they ask most frequently, but I spare them the details of this one. It would snuff out the bright neon light in their eyes.

January 30th – Dr Jonathan Nylon

Oh God – the public library – the stench of urine, Bovril and stale cologne seeping from between the pages of germ-infested tomes. Actions that you would assume can only be performed in a single way, can in fact be carried out in multiple, unpredictable and peculiar ways, when taking place in a public library. Browsing for a book for example. During my visit this morning, I came across a man standing over a table of miscellaneous books in the middle of the foyer. He was staring straight ahead and picking up the books from the top of the piles with both hands and then dropping them back down again, without reading anything. Is this the correct way to engage with books? I think not. They ought to consider launching a literature engagement scheme to improve the situation.

I managed to source a couple of tomes on Genghis Khan, one entitled *The Leadership Secrets of*

Genghis Khan, which I hope will also be useful for teaching the drama students. I also swiped a copy of *The Wandsworth Women's Health book: a guide to Women's Health and Well-being,* to gen up on ways to stay healthy during these uncertain times – it's dated from 1997 and obviously gender specific, but they didn't have much in the way of books on general health. A man emerged from behind the shelving unit of the Health Section whilst I was mid-perusal and staggered erratically towards me clutching Ian Wright's autobiography. I tried to use it as a buffer, but it was a paperback version in an acetate cover, and it slipped from his grasp. He clung to me like a dying man and coughed directly into my face, unable to shield me with his hands. It was a shocking and unsettling moment. His last words to me were, 'Where is *Squirrel Nutkin* 599.360'. I don't know if he was searching for a book or an MI5 agent. Aid eventually came in the form of the library assistant, who removed the books he had tripped over and offered him some water to sober him up. I stayed long enough to see the

338

gentleman come to – but I lost precious hand washing time in doing so. Good God! I shall be in my grave by sunrise. Yes, the crow does fly east and he's bringing his vulture friend with him.

11 pm – just been for a drink with George at the *Sylvan Post*. He has been promoted to Senior Reporter, although he fears he's not doing enough to ensure the security of his position. Adjusting to the casual banter of the senior staff is proving difficult for him. He attempted to throw his hat in the banter ring during a kitchen gathering the other day. 'It was awful, Johnny,' he said, 'the Editor made a joke about covering a story in a dicey part of Docklands and pretended to pull out a gun. I ran out the kitchen in mock shock. But everyone just thought I was running because I had some work to do. I'm having to run everywhere now, just to keep up the charade! It's exhausting – in every way.' I was listening, dear diary, but my thoughts are flooded with fears of contracting

coronavirus at the moment, and George tends to get quite close when telling a tale. Bobby has developed a dry cough of late as well. Thank God, he keeps himself in self-imposed quarantine as a matter of course. I had a vision of myself, in lockdown with Bobby – scouring the dark web in search of hand sanitiser, civilians stockpiling thermometers (one for every orifice). I aired my concerns with the old folks the other day, and it launched them into a debate over who would survive, should an outbreak occur in the UK. Eunice seemed more concerned with her new downstairs toilet being completed than her full lifespan.'I don't care if he has to wear a full white bodysuit, Gary's coming in to finish that bleeding bathroom,' she said.

I hope we will still be able to get fresh fruit and veg if things do worsen – Bobby is getting through my supplies at a rate of knots. He's taken to dating women in the hallway at the moment. He seems to have two on rotation – they sit in the cupboard and watch the same film, gorging themselves on overspiced vegetable curries. Always the same film, makes me think of that German tradition of watching *Dinner for One.*

I came out of my room the other night and Girl 1 was eating a mango and there was half a cucumber on the table with a knife next to it. I emerged later in the evening and was forced to skirt past the foldout garden table he'd erected in the middle of the hallway to get to the toilet. During which I spotted that the lovers had relocated to 'Bobby's room', door wide open. They were sat bolt upright, side by side, like two children on the front of a 1970s board game box. At the end of the night, there was an extended discussion about who would take the cucumber portion home – I was relieved for her sake, he insisted it be her, I think she needed it more than him. He is an odd sort of lothario. I hope these characters won't be moving in on a permanent basis.

We won't be able to sustain them with a balanced diet – my fresh veg would be the first to go and Bobby's food shelf is permanently and solely populated by a vat of kombucha. We'd have to live off his tincture and homegrown herbal teas. I expressed my concerns to George. We drank six more pints and a hot toddy each – belt and braces.

1 am – just making a note to make a note to post in the library comments box: a request for surgical- style foot and hand washing basins positioned at the library entrance. I hope she takes this one seriously at least.

January 30th – Dr Molly Beaujolais

Letter from 'Joel' delivered with burger grease stains on the corners. I knew it.

Molly,

How are you baby cakes? I hope this finds you well and that mean old manager isn't working you too hard. You asked me in your letter previous if I am a writer. Well, as it so happens, I am! And I've been working on something in here. I wonder if you would mind telling me what you think?

Joel x

PS: *Book has no pictures at the moment, could you send me some snaps for inspiration?*

Prepared a letter enclosed with an etching of a dour-looking Midwest woman from the 1800s and a couple of chalk nudes I found in a drawer in the bunker – nude-headed bald eagles that is. I accidentally spilled a split glowstick on the lady's hair – but he'll probably enjoy that – makes her look more like a computer animation.

10 pm – the courier has just come into the box office and asked if I want to see what he's been working on. 'Just a few letters,' he said and then spelt out 'drink?' in glowsticks on the counter. He struggled with the question mark of course, but I'm assuming it was a question and he's not just an alcoholic expressing himself through craft. I had my suspicions, but I am

still shocked by the charade. I thought courtship was complicated in England! A drink may do me good, however – especially a free one. Put some colour back in my cheeks. Johnny's absence has drained me. I walked past a dead slowworm the other day and felt absolutely nothing. Well, it turned out to be a piece of rubber that had been holding some scaffolding together, but all the same. My heart is ice cold. I told the courier he owes me several drinks. He asked me how he could ever repay me. I said, 'you could buy a ticket, they're worth their weight in blood, sweat, tears and gold.' He said he would rather live to see our grandchildren grow up.

February 1st – Dr Jonathan Nylon

Well Brexit is upon us, and I feel the same. Thank God. I was convinced I was going to die in the night after that library episode. I've splashed out on an NHS therapy session, to try and 'process' some of the latest goings on – 90 quid it's cost me! I had a call with someone on a helpline beforehand and we talked about the potential for poetry to open me up a bit and let some feelings loose. I've composed one about the student admirer to get the juices flowing. (Not a euphemism!)

His feelings are like wild animals
A rabbit with myxomatosis
Every time I picture his face
I picture Glenn Close
Too close for comfort
Then the credits rolling
The credits to my life

She also recommended I put together a 'worry box' of precious items that will always be sure to spark feelings of joy and peace. I've put Molly's poem in there – and hand sanitiser.

February 3rd – Dr Molly Beaujolais

Shared a burger with 'Joel'. We talked all things art, music and upholstery. I have to admit, I prefer these apples to those onions.

February 4th – Dr Jonathan Nylon

'For the rain it raineth every day'. It pissed down at

The Globe and none of the drama students had coats. The tour guide looked at me like a neglectful parent.

They did look like they'd been mugged on the tube,

but I'd like to think I don't possess the look of the

kind of man who would allow them to

Step-Ball-Change into the path of a band of brigands without stepping in.

I spoke to McKinney yesterday about procuring the stage, but he was not forthcoming. I'll have to ask about – they are very keen to perform. It is

an awkward situation. I don't know what to say to them

when they perform in front of me. I mean, is it OK, Dido? Probably not is the honest answer.

The tour guide gave a fascinating account of The Globe's history, but it was not enough to occupy the minds of my students apparently. There was a lot of flirtatious mucking about with the ponchos. I was pleasantly surprised – they all got on like a house on fire in fact – a Jacobean theatre on fire!

I've roped the history lot into helping out backstage for the play and assigned some marketing duties. I thought I might get a moment to myself at lunch, but Dido remained at my side like a faithful cur. He asked me for a task, so I playfully suggested a bark rubbing of one of the wooden pews. He came back 10 minutes later saying they didn't have any crayons at the box office, but he'd found a postcard with a tree on it from a production of *A Midsummer Night's Dream*, he said he liked the poem (Theseus's speech on lovers and madmen) and would that do? It'll do for now, until I can find him some proper psychiatric help.

It continued to pour cats and curs for the performance of *The Taming of the Shrew*. It was a brilliant show, although it was a strain to make out the

Shakespearean words and meaning with the old lady sat next to me's induction loop amplifying the rain into my right ear. I suppose it all added to the atmosphere – angst and rising tension.

February 6th – Dr Molly Beaujolais

Work on the set build continues – the number of rooms and actor casualties grows each day. It is like a re-enactment of the construction of the Winchester Mystery House of San Jose, the manager is Idaho's version of William Wirt – attempting to atone for the bloodshed. Luce is considering jacking it in – the set is never going to be secure, and neither are our pay cheques. 'Joel' aka Kevin Bernard has very kindly offered to lend us a stipend. He suggested we take the scaffolding to build our own ark like Noah in *The Notebook.* I'm not sure what animals he is seeing to put in it. All I see is onions – in my waking and dreaming life. He asked me if I've seen the film and I said, 'Have I missed the reference? We are on different planes.' To which he replied, 'no matter, we will be on the same waters soon.' I should probably take him up on it. Luce is right, I don't think we will be in business long. A fire inspector took a tour of the site yesterday and deemed it 'a death trap'. It's in his notes, in black and white – black, white and red.

11 pm – Kevin revealed to me this evening that he is a descendant of someone he refers to as 'the bestie guy in art' – an art dealer by trade. He is bestie buds with all the cool cats – perhaps they can join us on the ark!

February 8th – Dr Jonathan Nylon

Joleen called round to check on Bobby today. She brought the two hounds with her, and I offered to take them for a spin in Regent's Park. I left before she'd made contact with Bobby in his toxic bunker. 'She'll be fine,' I thought, she seems like a horsey type. The dogs had waterproof jackets to put on, the greyhound resembled a wad of parchment slotted into a school ziplock folder. It was not the relaxing experience I had anticipated. Actually, the park was packed – I looked longingly at a patch of green across the way, which I should've chosen. It was practically deserted, a few stick people dotted about the plain like an unfinished Lowry sketch – taunting me. I watched that film about him recently, all those masterpieces burnt to a crisp – he must have felt a similar feeling, gazing into the flames. The pug pestered me continually to throw a ball I did not possess, despite me emptying my pockets and explaining at length that I didn't have one. Molly would have enjoyed the surrealist monologue I orated on my way: 'This is not a ball. The ball does not exist.'

This is not a life. Life does not exist – without her.

February 10th – Dr Molly Beaujolais

Kevin continues to surprise me! He tells me that his family own the real-life Hans Holbein portrait of Henry VIII. I want to tell Johnny.

February 11th – Dr Jonathan Nylon

Bobby has given me his dry cough. Another reason to feel frustration towards him, besides the unbearable slowness of his being. I can find no remedy for Bobby in *The Wandsworth Women's Health Book: A Guide to Women's Health and Well-being*. Even the smallest action such as stirring a cup of tea is carried out with ceremonial slowness. He keeps leaving the spoons everywhere, as well – there's one long brass one, he particularly favours. I don't know whether he's using it for opium or Lemsip. Should I wash it with Fairy Liquid or bleach? This is how Genghis Khan must have felt whenever he had a cold.

He is causing me to develop an utter intolerance of slow-paced individuals. An elderly gentleman walked in front of me three times on the Underground the other day – once at the platform and then again by the escalator. By the time we got to the barriers, and he tried to intercept me again, I almost blurted out 'you and me are going to fall out in a minute'. I could actually feel the words forming on my lips.

My faith in old people was restored later in the day, however, as Leslie Jumbo has said we can use the allotment for the play – he has a gazebo and everything. I've sent out invitations to Molly's friends and family and one to her New York address.

February 12ᵗʰ Molly Beaujolais

Kevin has persuaded me to reach out to the real Joel Jericho Souris. He is remorseful about his deception and feels Joel the original should not be deprived of my good will and sweet nature. He says there is enough of it to fill an ebony and bronze Louis XVI desk once owned by Paderewski with love filled letters. I'm not sure Boise Prison will be furnishing their inmates with such luxury, but it was a nice image.

February 14th – Dr Molly Beaujolais

The letter is sent. I had to condense everything into the one submission, so it is quite lengthy – I also included some samples of my literary work and a collage of landmarks from around the UK and Europe. It is a day for love. And an evening for something like it – a diner dinner with Kevin and Luce. Maybe it's just the lukewarm heat from the griddle, but I feel I am warming to Kevin. And Johnny has a new love now – it is time to move on.

February 15th – Dr Jonathan Nylon

I think we have had a breakthrough with the play. I felt quite proud watching them frolicking dramatically about the cabbage patch today – they call it 'getting a feel for the space'. They forgot most of their lines, but they coped well with the rough terrain, which is half the battle. I think it's coming together. They did a grand job combatting the weeds as well. Act II of 'Operation Performance/Paraquat' will play out tomorrow.

11 pm – I am desperate to share the good news with Molly. Tried calling, but it went straight to voicemail.

February 17th – Dr Molly Beaujolais

Cracks are beginning to show in the Zomzooville franchise. The manager's business plan consists solely of ramping the prices up at an exponential rate – on the hour, every hour in fact. His idea of a lottery that costs more to enter than the prize money on offer is also failing to take hold. Customer numbers are dwindling – as is morale among the actors. When they first started flyering to draw in the crowds, they were positively bouncing off the non-existent walls in their attempts to entice the people of Peck to 'zap some zombies'. I heard one has modified his speech to 'anybody want to kill some people?' Nobody said no, in fairness.

February 18th – Dr Jonathan Nylon

Can't stop reading Molly's poem. She is the best woman I ever never had. Some very pretty lexical choices and metaphors – how I inspired them, I don't know. Why must my love life be a metaphor for the bleakness of life – I wonder if Wendy knows what a metaphor is? 'My face is like a potato.' No, 'my face is a potato.'

February 19th – Dr Molly Beaujolais

Just got off the phone from Nan. Not the conversation I was hoping for by a French Mexican long drop! I mentioned the Henry Holbein and the Paderewski desk. Bestie guy is in fact the Beistegui – Charles Beistegui. There is a very strong chance that Kevin and I could be related. She says unless I want to face the same charges as Marie Antoinette and live a life of letters (legal letters), I better let go of the Louise XVI ebony and bronze writing desk.

February 20th – Dr Jonathan Nylon

Oh God, I think I have the virus. I've been off sick

with a temperature today! I've been watching a lot of a

cartoon called *Bing* – it follows on from *The Split* on

iPlayer. It's about a family of two out-of-proportion rabbits. It makes me think I could be a father. The disproportionately small Scottish patriarch does a terrible job. He goes along with Bing's suggestion of a night-walk through the streets just before bed, potentially dangerous, and, if he came across a night-dwelling character like Bobby, he'd never sleep again!

I'm not sure their relationship is a good model for familial bliss – Bing's and his minder's – one where one party frequently, yet surprisingly unintentionally, lures the other to his death. What do I know – maybe this is the secret to having a harmonious relationship? At least it would avoid an acrimonious break up.

In another episode, he asks Bing to try sitting down in a bathtub he has filled to the top, bordering on attempted murder that! Mark Rylance has such a kindly voice though, I think I'd go along with it.

If Molly asked me to immerse myself in a full bathtub, I would buy a subscription to the Lido and make it a daily ritual. To be with her – even for a half-day at the spa, I would endure a lifetime of 2-inch, tepid baths. I would be eternally happy then. But it will never be – she still won't return my calls and the council have turned our water off.

Perhaps I should sign up at the Lido, I could do with the exercise and access to clean water. It would have to be a singleton's membership; I couldn't have joint ownership of anything with Molly now. I was thinking one day I might be able to save up to pay the mortgage on her flat, and we could live happily ever after here. But I fear she would eventually take me to the cleaners, if we were to marry now. And not to wash our love-soaked sheets.

February 21st – Dr Molly Beaujolais

No word from Joel, Johnny or Jehovah. One word from my soul – forsaken. If only I had a roof terrace designed by Salvador Dali to throw myself off.

February 22nd – Dr Jonathan Nylon

357

Why won't Molly speak to me? I just want to know she's OK. The play is scheduled for six days' time. I don't know how I'll cope if she's not there.

February 27th – Dr Molly Beaujolais

Oh, dear God. I have received a letter from Joel's parole officer!

Dear Dr Molly Beaujolais,

I am not sure how you got hold of Joel's location here, but please refrain from contacting him. He is of a fragile state of mind and confesses to feeling 'harassed' by your recent letter. He says he has spent the majority of his life being harassed by women and he would like to spend his last days in peaceful isolation and singleness, working on his novel, 'Fred Wand and the Ice-Cream Maker's Cone', a tale of a boy with magic powers who is sent to a correctional facility that can only be accessed via underwater Chevrolets.

Your sincerely,

Luke Partridge

Oh God. Oh God. Oh God. Oh God!

February 28th – Dr Jonathan Nylon

Molly is here.

She called me from campus. She'd heard a report on the news that a man from England had fallen ill in a Tudor maze within a university facility and had had to be airlifted to safety. She said she thought it must be me, seeing as I don't go anywhere. I'm not sure what I should be more offended about, the fact that she thinks I am provincial or that I am sizeable enough to need to be airlifted to safety. I made a quick call to McKinney and discovered that the culprit is in fact Dr Branston – he'll be pickled in a jar and contributing to the new foyer cabinet display in no time!

I called her straight back. There was a lot of crying. She told me that she loves me. I asked her what she was wearing. She said, 'now is not the time.' I said, 'No, are you warm enough— meet me at the allotment.' She said something about harassing a convict and a collage that I didn't understand.

'He didn't enjoy my poems,' she said.

'He probably doesn't enjoy much, Molly,' I replied. 'The man is about to be executed.'

I knew then that this was a time to break out the big guns, Eskimo's twin QF 4.7-inch (120 mm) Mk XII guns. I grabbed the sauce pot sculpture for luck and headed to the theatre's rickety gates.

Leslie Jumbo greeted me in a red felt waistcoat as an usher. The players were all assembled. Molly stood by the gate. My beautiful Molly - a vision of absolute loveliness. In her white sheep jumper. She stayed glued to the spot this time, she wasn't wearing her running shoes - instead she had on one heeled boot - the other one had made its way through my office window apparently, in a desperate bid to make contact with me. Another thing to add to my list of expenses for this term. What a volte-farce, to use a theatre term! I died of happiness and the lovers died of something, it wasn't clear what because our budget was not vast.

Remarkably the performance went off without a hitch, with the exception of Dido forgetting to exit the stage on several occasions. Vasques handled the situation well with some improvised lines, 'who will rid me of this troublesome priest' among them. Giovanni and Annabella did a sterling job – Robert I'm sure is heading for the dazzling lights of Hollywood, he seemed to be squinting into them already in the 'One more Kiss' scene. He resembled an opportunist Mr Magoo putting the moves onto an unsuspecting optician's assistant. I found out later that Margot had been liberally distributing Bach Flower Remedy around the players, mixed with something or other, so that might have contributed to the array of bizarre facial expressions on display.

The audience seemed to enjoy it and there was a full house. Mostly friends and family, but a few faces I didn't recognise. An elderly gentleman that I later discovered to be Ralph Sotheby. He and Eunice were drawn to each other like two magnets, gracelessly and mechanically.

When the applause had died down, which didn't take long, I disappeared behind the greenhouse with Molly, and she asked me if she is 'too mad for love'. She said there is a point, and she always seems to go past it. The image of a scatter graph came into my head.

'Mad as a March hare,' she said. 'Mad as the Queen of Hearts?'

I said, 'No, mad as the Mad Hatter, that's you – making everyone tea in the asylum and getting them to sing round the piano.'

'Always too much of this and not enough of that, Johnny,' she said, sprinkling soil over a potato, like a faltering *Saturday Kitchen* contestant. Then she looked down, trying to re-plant her frozen potato in the cold, hard earth and I said something quite poetic and beautiful I think – about her. I don't even know where it came from. I wish I could remember it. All I remember is picking up the potato and hurling it as far as I possibly could, into the horizon.

And then I kissed her. Properly this time.

February 28th – Dr Molly Beaujolais

'Molly, you are a single dot on a very long and limitless horizon. And I don't mean limitless in a good, mystical way – I mean like a limitless amount of shite and disastrous consequences. You are Hawking's singular singularity. I can't look away even if I wanted to. You are a fixed thing. I just want to stand still with you – kneel down on this cold, horrible, hard soil – with you there. You make me feel that I can, that I want to do that! That I can do most things really. But I don't want to do any of it without you.'

'[...] hilarious [...] I couldn't get enough of these characters and raced through their appealingly crazy, uncensored internal monologues, wishing they could speak openly like this to each other. Different and moreish.' - Sarah Lawrence, Daily Mail

'I really enjoyed this. Funny, original and unexpectedly moving.' Harry Peacock ('Ray Purchase' in Toast of London)

'For anyone who has ever enjoyed Peep Show and that classically British cringe humour this is the perfect novel for you!' Harry McWhirter, Waterstones Bookseller

'Loved this book. Beckett with Hemingway overtones, and seasoned with remarkable humour:) A whirlwind love story unlike any other!' Tony

'It's a long time since I've laughed aloud so frequently reading a book but This Diary (World) Belongs to Molly and Johny made me snort with laughter time and again...What Laura Clark does so brilliantly is to explore the human condition, and the need we all have for connection and intimacy in a world gone mad...' - Linda's Book Bag

'The characters were so well written that I could have read this if it were 1000 pages. Witty and outrageously funny, it kept me smiling but it was also moving and realistic in our chaotic lives.' Brena Newnhan, Waterstones Bookseller

Printed in Dunstable, United Kingdom